SIXTY LIGHTS

Gail Jones teaches literature, cinema and cultural studies
at the University of Western Australia. She is the author
of two collections of short stories, *Fetish Lives* and *The
House of Breathing*, and one previous novel, *Black
Mirror*, which won the Nita B. Kibble Award.

Gail Jones

SIXTY LIGHTS

V

VINTAGE

Published by Vintage 2005

2 4 6 8 10 9 7 5 3 1

Copyright © Gail Jones 2004

Gail Jones has asserted her right under the Copyright, Designs
and Patents Act, 1988 to be identified as the author of this work

Eduardo Cadava quote reprinted by permission of the author

Walter Benjamin quote reprinted by permission of the publisher
from *The Arcades Project* by Walter Benjamin, trans. Howard
Eiland and Kevin McLaughlin, Cambridge, Mass.: The Belknap
Press of Harvard University Press, © 1999 by the President and
Fellows of Harvard College

First published in Great Britain in 2004 by
The Harvill Press

Vintage
Random House, 20 Vauxhall Bridge Road,
London SW1V 2SA

Random House Australia (Pty) Limited
20 Alfred Street, Milsons Point, Sydney
New South Wales 2061, Australia

Random House New Zealand Limited
18 Poland Road, Glenfield,
Auckland 10, New Zealand

Random House (Pty) Limited
Endulini, 5A Jubilee Road, Parktown 2193,
South Africa

The Random House Group Limited Reg. No. 954009
www.randomhouse.co.uk/vintage

A CIP catalogue record for this book
is available from the British Library

ISBN 0 099 47203 1

Papers used by Random House are natural, recyclable
products made from wood grown in sustainable forests.
The manufacturing processes conform to the environ-
mental regulations of the country of origin

Printed and bound in Great Britain by
Bookmarque Ltd, Croydon, Surrey

For my brothers, Peter and Kevin Jones

PART ONE

"There has never been a time without the photograph, without the residue and writing of light"

Eduardo Cadava

I

A VOICE IN THE DARK: "LUCY?"

It was a humid-sounding whisper. She wanted this, this muffled gentleness, swathed in sheets scented and moistened by the heated conjoining of their bodies. This tropic of the bed. This condensation of herself into the folds of a marriage. The late night air was completely still. Insects struck at the mosquito net, which fell, silver and conical, like a bridal garment around them. Lucy watched a pale spotted moth sail slowly towards her face, land on the net, deposit its powder, and lift unevenly away. It was waving like a tiny baby hand in the darkness.

This is what she had seen, earlier that day: An Indian man had been climbing the bamboo scaffolding of one of the high colonial buildings, with a large mirror bound to his body by a piece of cloth. His white dhoti was flapping and his orange turban was atilt, and he hauled himself with confidence from level to precarious level — altogether a fellow who knew what he was doing — when some particular gust or alarum that carried the dimension of fate caused him to misjudge his footing and fall through the air. Because he could not release the mirror, but clutched at it as though it was a magic carpet, he landed in the midst of its utter shattering, and was speared through the chest. The quantity of blood was astounding. It

3

spurted everywhere. But what Lucy noticed most – when she rushed close to offer assistance along with everyone else – was that the mirror continued its shiny business: its jagged shapes still held the world it existed in, and bits and pieces of sliced India still glanced on its surface. Tiny shocked faces lined along the spear, compressed there, contained, assembled as if for a lens. She simply could not help herself: she thought of a photograph.

And only later, in deep night, did Lucy rise in distress. She found herself bolt upright, staring at the darkness, and seeing before her this man who was horribly killed. He had died quickly, she supposed, because his black eyes were fixed open and his mouth was mutely agape, but there he was, halted in time. She saw the elements only now: the shade of the tamarind tree into which he fell, the lifting of startled crows in a flapping explosion, a woman who stood with her blue sari spattered bright red, the children who hurried forward to gather fragments of mirror, Bashanti, her servant, weeping into her dupatta. The community of the accident. The gory congregation. Two men appeared with sackcloth to carry away the body in a sling. Lucy remembered stepping backwards when she realised that blood was soaking her satin-covered boots, and seeing her own miniaturised face retreat and disappear.

In bed the man beside her turned over, half-awake. His dark humped shape set the mosquito net aquiver.

"Lucy?" he enquired again.

He sounded almost loving.

She will remember this utterance of her name when she meets her own death – in a few years' time, at the age of twenty-two. It will signify the gentleness that briefly existed between them. For now, however, she senses the baby stir

4

within her, aroused by her night terror and her pounding pulse, and feels entirely alone. She is stranded in this anachronistic moment she can tell no-one about, this moment that greets her with the blinding flash of a burnt magnesium ribbon.

2

IN 1860 THE EIGHT-YEAR-OLD CHILD, LUCY STRANGE, AND HER
brother Thomas, aged almost ten, were doubly orphaned. It
was during one of those Australian summers when the sky
was so fiery and brittle that it could barely sustain incursions
of flight, so that birds, sun-struck, fell dead to the ground.
Earth cracked open, flowers bleached and dropped away,
household dogs, their tongues lolling, lay panting on their
sides. The children returned from school to the lattice-shaded
verandah of their wooden house to discover their mother,
Honoria, stretched on a long wicker chair (a chair Uncle
Neville would later call a "Bombay fornicator"), fanning
herself and appearing as if some artist had tinted her face pink.
Her belly was enormous and seemed suddenly to have arrived:
the children had no recollection of it gradually growing. They
dimly apprehended the fact of pregnancy – or at least as
Thomas had worked it out, with cartoonish imprecision –
but it did not explain why Mama, who had been so sweetly
attentive, had become this rather heavy and irascible woman,
almost entirely immobile, who was so self-absorbed as barely
to acknowledge their existence. As they climbed the steps to
the verandah she paused in her fanning, smiled a half-smile,
but said nothing at all; they saw her reach for a glass of
cold water which she pressed against her cheek, rolling it

distractedly, back and forth. Tiny droplets of moisture adhered to her face.

Although on this day Lucy wished to approach and speak to her mother, she found herself hesitating. Instead she tickled the belly of her sprawled-out spaniel, Ned, and wondered how long she must wait here, in this blazing afternoon, looking at her mother's swollen bare feet, and the fan that now rested against her face, obscuring it in a deckle-edged circle of flowers. This fan imprints itself on Lucy's heart, for it is from this day that her life enters the mode of melodrama, and this little partition between them, of such oriental blue, will register for ever the vast distances that love must travel. *Duck-egg blue*, she will recall as an adult. *My mother's chysanthemum fan was duck-egg blue.*

Thomas called from inside and Lucy trailed away. She washed her face at the enamel basin and held it too long underwater without knowing why, her eyes open to the bubbles of her own expiration.

When at last it came, Honoria's birthing shuddered every space in the house. Mrs Minchin arrived, and later Doctor Stead, but Father must have known that even twenty midwives and doctors would not suffice. Honoria's cries were ragged and hysterical with premonitions of doom. The baby, a daughter, was born alive. It was yellow and ugly, Mrs Minchin told the children. They understood that it had been too newly formed to survive and that some vague meaty piece, part of its body, perhaps, had not broken away, but had stayed within their mother to poison and destroy her. Lucy was afraid of Mrs Minchin. She bore a purple birthmark that lay across one third of her face, so that she looked always to be moving in her own private shadow, and the girl, superstitious, took this stain as the sure sign of a more general darkening. Besides, this woman

7

knew such terrible things. She knew of bits of baby that might detach and go internally astray. She had carried swabs of bloody cloth from lying-in rooms to incinerators. She had held the jelly of foetuses and pressed the hands of dying women. She was a woman connected to transformations and negations of the body never quite spoken aloud. In the three days it took Honoria Strange to die, during which time the hectic blush travelled from her cheeks, down to her chest, and then to encompass her whole body, so that ice in canvas packs was applied everywhere to cool her, Lucy convinced herself that the midwife Mrs Minchin was to blame.

When news of the death came, it was Thomas, unsuperstitious, who burst into tears, and Lucy who was undisturbed and curiously composed, having already surrendered her mother to the power of the birthmarked shadow. Ned commenced a long and sorry howling. Father shut himself away in the bedroom. Then Thomas, embarrassed and at a loss, disappeared for a whole day. So Lucy was left to wander alone in the parched garden where she plucked at dried flower-heads and crumbled them between her fingers, and watched dusty light shift and fluctuate across the dead grass. She tried to trap skinks and crickets under upturned flowerpots, so she could burn them with her magnifying glass. Finding no animals or insects, she burnt holes in her smock. It satisfied her, this brief destructive concentration. She liked the smoke, the tiny flame, the appearance of a black-ringed hole – all those fiery perforations that damaged the cloth so irreparably. It was like being a criminal; Lucy felt the serious pleasure of doing something forbidden. The chickens in the pen watched her, their amber eyes stupid. Lucy ran at them and shook the wire so that she could see them scatter. She swung her magnifying glass as if it was a deadly weapon. She hated the chickens because they pecked at her knees when she fed them, and because they knew.

In the house, bereavement settled as an abstract quality of distortion. For some reason Mrs Minchin, a childless widow, had been invited to stay; her deplorable presence made Lucy rather silent and disengaged. She would not talk to this woman, nor would she look at her. Thomas also acquired an isolating intensity, devoting himself to self-enclosing regimes of study. From the Mechanics Institute he brought home books on electrics, astronomy, biology and railways. He seemed to have forgotten about his sister and his childhood, and worked away emphatically, like an over-industrious adult. As to their father: he was absent; he was unrecognisable. He did not get up each morning, as he had done for years, to catch the horse-drawn tram to the Bank of Australasia, but stayed hidden in the house, lingering in the musty bedroom in which his wife had died. Lucy caught a glimpse of him once, in a wedge of disclosure, when Mrs Minchin took him a jug of water. It was late in the afternoon and he was sitting on the edge of his bed, hunched over, hands clasped together, dressed only in brown-and-white striped pyjama bottoms. Tea-coloured light illuminated one side of his face, and with his yellow complexion and unshaven aspect he looked like one of the tramps near the hotel that her mother had warned her about. Moreover his skin had developed some kind of rash; his forearms and chest were coloured crimson. The child was scandalised. As she lay on the verandah with Ned, her face buried in his fur, she thought of the dozens of ways in which she might murder Mrs Minchin. In the periphery of her vision lay the long wicker chair on which she imagined her mother, still pregnant, intangibly returned.

A few hours before his death, Father emerged with bloodshot eyes, dishevelled and suddenly old, from the funereal bedroom, and beckoned to his children. He propped Lucy on his lap and bade Thomas stand close beside his rose-velvet armchair; and then with flat stilted speeches made farewell presentations. Thomas must always look after his little sister, and he must take possession of a gold watch, once owned by his grandfather, and keep it tucked against his chest as a talisman of family pride. Lucy must take an ornate Italian locket, within which rested a silhouetted, cut-paper profile of her mother, purchased in Florence during her honeymoon. "The image is precious," he said. "Keep it always." Father's ceremonial manner disconcerted the children; they exchanged perplexed glances – uncomprehending – and wriggled to be free. Lucy recoiled from the foul smell of her father's pyjamas, and realised with disgust that he had not bothered to wash. The rash on his body made him appear diseased and in his hand the pretty Italian locket looked tarnished and grimy. She hid it in the bookcase, behind *Bleak House*.

When he took rat poison, Arthur Strange understood, above all, the abasement of his own grief and his shameful refusal to endure for the sake of his children. A simple and savage desperation took hold of him. He swallowed the vile substance and thought of nothing in particular. Death was dull, it was drab, it was solitude confirmed. For the occasion of his death Arthur had been untypically well organised. He wrote a short formal letter to the Bank of Australasia, another to his father, and one to his brother-in-law, Neville, but nothing to his children. What words could explain the blasted hollow his wife's death had carved in him? Thomas was numbed, Lucy was relieved, and Mrs Minchin, her purple face livid, became mobilised, almost jaunty, with the extra responsibility. She laundered anew the mourning suits the children had worn two weeks before, her large body swift and efficient, her manner professional. It was, Lucy reflected, as if this woman had absorbed the human energy that once belonged to her parents. Mrs Minchin had thick fingers and moved household objects abruptly. She instructed, took control.

The day of the second funeral was sweltering. The priest's garments were discoloured with circular patterns of sweat and he kept pausing in his speech to mop his brow. The children joked about it later, with miserable humour. A man from the bank said their father had been A Decent and Upstanding Citizen, Felled by Tragedy.

It may have been a fantasy, or perhaps it was a dream: Lucy had intervened to prevent her mother's death.

When Honoria was coral-pink and burning with poison, Lucy had taken ice and a spoon and a candle to light the way, curled up very small, small as a new baby, and squeezed, eyes closed, into her mother's belly. She had scooped out the fleshy matter that caused such harm, and then slept there a while, her job well done, within the snug crimson dome of her mother's secret insides. In this netherland she was absolutely cool and comfortable. She sucked on ice, and rolled it in a glass against her cheek. The little candle, unwavering, shone on and on. Casting out every threatening and mystifying shadow.

3

TO EVOKE A FACE, IN ALL ITS PRECISION, IS VERY DIFFICULT, BUT FOR a long time afterwards Honoria Brady thought about the precise moment in which she met her future husband, Arthur Strange. It was so suffused with romance, so *face to face*. She had been travelling on the coach from Melbourne to Geelong, and had open before her a copy of the novel *Jane Eyre*, so that she was busy imagining the unhappy estrangement of lovers. No thing distracted her, not the old woman asleep opposite, her fat eyelids flickering, nor the marmalade kitten the woman had brought with her, scratching at the walls of its tight basket. Not the smoky light, since it was still early morning, nor the jolting rhythms and vibrations of the vehicle she travelled in. The landscape fled by in a disintegrating blur, and the compartment Honoria inhabited was not this wood-panelled and glass-paned one, rattling along the road, but her own quiet space, with its own duration and propulsion. She travelled *Jane Eyre*. She was sped on by its melancholy and motivating desire.

I am Jane Eyre, she secretly told herself. *I am honourable but unnoticed. I am passionate and strong. I need a lover who will carry my future in the palm of his hand.*

The coach accident was a minor one: the two horses shied and swerved at something unexpected, and with a single swift jerk the coach flipped onto its side. Honoria was thrown forward upon the bosom of the sleeping woman, who woke screaming and frantic with disorientation. The woman would not be calmed; she had no idea where she was, and thrashed about, upsetting her cat basket and knocking hard against the window. Outside were shouts and exclamations and the anxious whinnying of horses, but a man came running very fast, attracted by the screams. He bobbed, jumping, then heaved himself to the window, and gestured that the door be opened. When Honoria pushed the chestnut frame upwards she was only inches from his face. His eyes were large and glistening with the possibility of tragedy; she could see small flecks of bronze in their blue, and the pupils expanding.

"Is she hurt?" he asked. "I'm coming in."

With that he hauled himself towards her, sliding on his stomach through the aperture, and was suddenly there, reaching in, lifting the woman under the armpits. Honoria pushed from behind, and together they manoeuvred her safely to the ground. The young man then held up his arms and Honoria, kneeling now with the kitten basket on the side of the upturned coach, simply slid into them. For the smallest moment he encircled her narrow waist, then turned his attention again to the older woman. Instinctively he brushed back a loose wisp of her hair: Honoria was moved by the purity of the gesture and by the shape of his large hand.

"Just a fright," he murmured. "Just a little fright."

Honoria reached for the kitten, arched in alarm, and was scratched in parallel lines on the wrist for her trouble. Gallantly, the young man produced a white handkerchief. He settled the old lady, summoned a cup of tea from an onlooker and then – unnecessarily, since it was so faint an injury – wrapped the cloth, monogrammed "A", around Honoria's thin wrist. It was only then that he looked at her. She was about seventeen, plain, her skin rather bluish in the early morning light, yet she carried about her an aura of erotic intensity, as though she had travelled with special knowledge from a foreign country. The young man looked away again, and fiddled with the knot of the handkerchief.

"Honoria Brady," she announced, and proffered her unscratched hand.

"Arthur Strange, Coach Driver."

Honoria realised she had not even looked at him when she boarded the coach, or at his boy assistant, now unharnessing and calming the horses.

"Edith MacMillan, Mrs," said the lady behind them. "And Camille, the kitten."

They were already a couple. They were already wed. Edith MacMillan, Mrs, their oversized cupid, paid for the honeymoon to cement her role in their happy collision.

Arthur Strange was twenty-two years old and lived in Geelong with his beloved father and stepmother. The son of Methodist missionaries, he had been born in Shanghai, China, where his mother had died of cholera two days before his eighth birthday. In an anguished crisis of faith his father, James, had suddenly quit his vocation and moved with his only son to live in Australia. They had initially settled in Sydney, where James had taken up building jobs to support his son, before meeting a tea merchant from the Toishen district in Kwantung province, who had travelled from Hong Kong and by odd circumstances ended in a tea shop in Swanston Street. Relieved to be once again speaking Cantonese, relieved to find a community of fellow souls – since James ineluctably felt more Chinese than European – he fell into partnership with Ah Chou and eventually married his daughter, Fen. It was a new beginning. Arthur adored Fen, not least for her cooking, but also because she made his father happy. A queen of the abacus, she doubled

14

James's business, doted on her husband, but to their mutual disappointment was unable to bear a child. The European community considered the family absurd (*strange by name, strange by nature*), and the marriage was regarded as somewhat perverse; certainly it ruined Arthur's chances with many of the local women. But he had accepted his loneliness with equanimity, and at the age of eighteen taken a position as a coach driver, which kept him so much in motion, and so unlocatable and inconspicuous, that he would not need to show the world how ungrounded he was.

Honoria Brady was the accident he had given up hoping for.

Because he now lived in Geelong, and she in Melbourne, their courtship took place at the Melbourne coach house, in the hour, each weekday, between the coach arriving and returning. Under arches of steel ornamented with fluttering pigeons, and in the hustle and bustle of travel, of ticket-finding and luggage-carting, Arthur and Honoria exchanged their intimacies. No place in Australia had ever been so ardent; Honoria centred her day on the coach that arrived for just her; Arthur rode not to Melbourne, but solely to Honoria. Their first kiss coincided with the blowing of a whistle; it was something they joked about for years to come.

The impediment was her father. George Brady was a widower, embittered and mean and he worked as the manager of a bank so that he could practise his meanness daily and with professional aplomb. The pride and joy was Neville, his son in the Indian Civil Service, but he considered his wayward daughter a flirt and a flibbertigibbet. He had chosen a colleague, a decent fellow, whom he considered a suitable match, but Honoria was ungovernable and disobedient. In the end he agreed to the marriage on the condition that this Arthur chap move to live in Melbourne and take up a position, one with real prospects, in a branch of his bank. Arthur readily agreed. He would have agreed to anything. He would have scaled the volcano Krakatoa if Honoria had been the prize. He would have swum to Tasmania to capture her kiss. At the wedding, to which Mrs Edith MacMillan and her husband were invited, George Brady was shocked by Arthur Strange's unconventional parents — he could not bring himself to acknowledge them, a Chinawoman and a Crank — but by then it was too late. Arthur and Honoria were inseparable. George resolved to make their lives a misery until grandchildren arrived.

Edith MacMillan held herself splendidly responsible for the Strange romance. She was eccentric and wealthy, and presented the delighted newlyweds with a card containing Camille's paw print, stamped in Indian ink, and a double sea passage to Italy so that they could honeymoon on the Continent. George Brady disapproved. He snorted into his beer and imagined shipwrecks.

Rocked on the ocean, then, in their own marital vehicle. Transported on scalloped waters and surging currents.

On their first night together Honoria told her lover Arthur Strange the entire plot of Charlotte Brontë's famous novel, *Jane Eyre*. Her triangle-shaped face lit up as she spoke. She was impassioned, fixated; she knew whole paragraphs by heart.

Arthur listened to the ocean wash against his new wife's voice. Thought Rochester a fool. Doted. Made a future. Fell at last into her warm body as if he were arriving somewhere safely, bathed in a white light from who-knows-where.

4

"I WANT YOU TO HAVE THIS. IT'S ALL I HAVE OF MY FIRST MOTHER."

"It's beautiful. Chrysanthemums. Tell me the story."

"The story?"

"You know. Where it came from, how she found it."

Arthur looked at his hands. He had never been asked for his stories before.

"When she first went to China," he began very quietly, "my mother was afraid. She feared illness, the people. She feared the foreignness of it all. A woman – not a Christian convert, but some sort of medicine woman she consulted – gave her the gift of this chrysanthemum fan. This woman told her through a translator that it was a special gift, and that she must use it to cool herself if she contracted fever or met Demon Spirits. It would protect her, the woman said."

Arthur's hands in his lap seemed to grow smaller.

"I think", he added tentatively, "that my mother believed it. In her last illness, I remember, she insisted that it be present. She was too weak with fever to raise her own hand, so my father held the fan. She thought she would recover. She smiled up at the fan. Its shadow waved slowly across her face . . . I saw her, like that, with the shadow moving . . . And what about your mother? Do you have a story?"

Honoria paused.

"I was really too young to remember my mother. And my father, in any case, would never speak of her. My brother Neville says he remembers the shape of her dresses. Like lampshades, he says. Like illuminated shades. He doesn't remember her face, though he must have been five when she died . . ."

(A lampshade. A hoop-shape around an untellable story.)

5

AMONG THE FORMS OF HER DILIGENT REVENGE, LUCY TOOK TO
burning small holes in Mrs Minchin's clothes. Mrs Minchin
was bewildered; she thought a moth of some kind, or even a
rat, was responsible. In the evening she patched what Lucy had
destroyed in the morning; the children watched her sew in
the chair that had not long before been their mother's.

The weeks after the deaths were almost unendurable. Apart
from the dreary satisfactions of tormenting Mrs Minchin,
Thomas and Lucy existed in a state of effacement and disability,
as though they shared an undiagnosable illness. A kind of
anaesthetic quality smothered their experience; they were
disengaged in each task they performed, and their feelings,
such as they were, were delayed and denuded. Moreover, the
children had become convinced that there were ghosts in the
house, presences that seemed everywhere to call: *behold me!* At
night they saw flitting shapes and weird transparencies. Noises
like whispers filled up the darkness. Once Thomas swore he
saw his father's face – unshaven, eyes bloodshot – hovering
on the surface of the hallway mirror; and Lucy dreamed that
the baby that would have been their sister was crawling in the
cramped, dark space beneath her bed. There was no vacancy
to grief. There were instead these drastic invasions, that hung
omnipresent in the air itself.

The children were relieved when Grandpa James sent coach tickets to visit him. He had not attended the funerals because he was confined to a wheelchair; and besides, he too had this undiagnosable condition. But he had written several times, and they had several times replied, and something in their tone and their scant news told him that they would be better out of the haunted house. As the coach pulled away the children ignored Mrs Minchin's solicitous wave. Ned, left behind, howled and howled. Mrs Minchin held him by the collar as he strained to follow.

When they are adults they will understand that this trip was a redemption; it saved whatever still existed after the corrosions of grief, after the dreadful threat to the children of unstill ghosts. Grandpa James had an illness that made his body tremble, but he was still pleased beyond measure that the children had come to stay.

"It's joy," he declared. "I'm weeping with joy."

James now lived with Fen in the mining town of Ballarat. He had settled on the goldfields and opened a small general store, mostly servicing the community of Chinese diggers. He sold picks, pots and pans, clothing, canvas tents, and assorted day-to-day and mining implements. In return he was offered genuine friendship — such as he had never experienced as a missionary — and a supply of fresh vegetables, including luxurious ginger. With his second wife at his side he had believed himself blessed. But now James could not balance these gifts against the deaths of Arthur and Honoria. No calculation or figuring sufficed. He deplored his own sense of fatality and doom, his own unholy feelings of emptiness. He wanted to ask his lost God forgiveness for his survival. The children stepped down from the coach and James greeted them, weeping.

Fen busied herself making elaborate Chinese confectionery, and invited her younger nieces and nephews, four in all, to the house to play. At first Thomas and Lucy were disconcerted by such attention — they had never before sat with so many faces around the table, or heard so much talk, some of it incomprehensible, or seen so many dishes arrayed before them; and all presided over by a woman who dressed every day in fabrics that shone like glass.

But they came to cherish this time, in this exotic household. It was, Thomas announced, like a new beginning. They ate new food, and met new people and did wholly new things: *life after death*. Grandpa James patiently taught both children to play chess — they had to move the pieces for him, so that his trembles would not upset the arrangements of the board — and Fen, with equal patience, taught them bridge and mahjong. In the tiny operations of castles and tiles, of horses and playing cards, in those dwarf obsessive circuits and friendly competitions, they all found distraction.

Among the cousins Lucy met an especial friend; she was Su-Lin, a pretty girl who was almost her age. They would curl up together under the low scented branches of the lemon tree, pretending they were twins, and sharing secrets. Su-Lin had honey-coloured skin and gold rings in her ears, and Lucy was in love with her. They agreed to marry when they were grown up, and have many, many children, but in the meantime Lucy showed her how to use the magnifying glass to burn her own name in pieces of wood. *Su-Lin*, in Chinese characters, appeared on the gatepost in front of the house; and James and Fen, amused, could not bring themselves to scold her. Thomas was also in love with Su-Lin: he did cartwheels to attract her attention and caught good-luck crickets for her straw cage and years later Lucy discovered that Su-Lin had also promised marriage to her brother.

In the evenings the children wheeled their grandfather down the main street of Ballarat. He hailed complete strangers and smiled at everyone. And now that he was ill, and had lost his son, and was grievously afflicted, most people were kinder and some smiled back.

It was a shock to learn that Uncle Neville, their mother's only brother, was travelling all the way from India to collect them. Grandpa James said it was what their father had wanted. He had, Grandpa James insisted, written and arranged it. So when the time was near the children were moved again. Their new beginning ended. They boarded the coach to Melbourne, back to the haunted house, and to purple-faced Mrs Minchin. At the coach house, their grandfather was trembling all over; his head was shaking like a puppet and he was weeping shamelessly. The cousins were there and so was Fen. Lucy and Thomas watched their family diminish to chesspiece size, until in the distance all that was visible was an oriental garment that caught the sun's rays and glittered, like a tube of lit glass.

6

THE HOUSE LOOKED CLOSED UP, BUT THEY KNEW MRS MINCHIN WAS there. Although the gate was looped with its rusty chain and the curtains were drawn, they could hear the sound of Ned, frantic at their return, leaping and barking in the hallway, running back and forth, testing the limits of his closed space with manic excitement. When they knocked there was an explosion of barking and scratching, but no Mrs Minchin came hurrying to answer the door. The children stood hand in hand on their own doorstep, like characters in a fairy tale, wondering what to do.

"Perhaps she's died," Lucy said hopefully.

"Murdered, I should think. With her throat cut," Thomas added. "And purple blood in bucketsful."

The boy was appalled by what he had just said. The children looked at each other, a little uncertain, and decided to consult the next-door neighbour.

Mrs O'Connor was blind and witchy and had hairs sprouting in a tiny neat plume from a mole on her cheek. She reached out for the children in case they were imposters, but they stood apart, and were ready to run if she grabbed at them.

"Thursday. She thinks it's Thursday that you're coming. She's up at Castlemaine, visiting her sister."

Her narrow hands hung in the air, both in threat and supplication, willing the children to move forward and consent to be touched. They looked like dead things, suspended there, so grey and shrivelled. Lucy thought: people die in different stages, this woman first in the eyes and then in the hands; and Thomas thought: she is dead already, she is like a mummy from Egypt, artificially preserved. The children were no less afraid for being beyond her reach.

"That poor, poor dog," Mrs O'Connor said. "Day and night it's been crying."

Thomas remembered his manners, and knew how to be formal.

"Thank you very kindly for the information, Mrs O'Connor. Most useful. Indeed."

And they ran off, back to their yard, and found the small square window, just near the kitchen chimney, that they knew could be forced. Thomas hoisted his sister up so that she stood balanced barefoot upon his shoulders, then she pushed, slid in on her belly, and he heard her plop down inside, accompanied by the yelps of Ned, now maddened with joy.

What was it in that pushing into shadows, so laden with dog-smell and must and the sour remains of foodstuffs (or was it the metallic taint of spilt blood or the emanations of ghost breath?); what was it in the simple dropping down and the dog leaping up that was still so terrifying? Lucy half expected to find Mrs Minchin dead, her neck cut open, her brown eyes staring, the sticky mess of a murder soaking their Turkish carpet. But it was not that at all. It was that she had never before been alone in their house, or seen it so closed. The stench, Lucy discovered, was of mutton and dog mess: Mrs Minchin had left a pile of bones for the dog, and a bucketful of water – *purple blood in bucketsful* – and locked it inside. Lucy held her nose and looked around her. In the unlit kitchen familiar objects asserted a new kind of strangeness. The curtains with their twining ivyleaf print. The erect, looming chairs. The scratched surface of the table and the doily at its centre. The milk jug appeared enormous and very solid. Lucy could see blue beads glinting on its white lacy cover. She felt she must not touch anything; these belonged to somebody else. And in the drawing room this effect of distance persisted: the armchairs, the bureau, the standing lamp with the shade that ended in a bobbled flare – these objects disturbed her with their alien quality of autonomy. She made her way to the front of the house, skirting the furniture, and when she opened the front door Ned flew out before her as though shot from a cannon. Thomas almost fell as the dog leapt at him, frenzied with recognition.

That first evening the children lay facing each other, on their parents' double bed. They heard the sound of corrugated iron contracting in the cool of the night, the wind from the east stirring in the wattle by the window, the chickens settling down, their querulous throaty murmurs. Ned was on the floor, unrelaxed, his bony head cocked. They were a three-some afraid. As it grew darker, Thomas and Lucy talked quietly for a while but did not go to their own rooms or light the lamps. They undressed in the gathering darkness and slept very early, with their thin arms and legs bound in a wreath-shape, together.

Lucy dreamed a vague dream in which she was trapped in a confined space. There was the sound of wind blowing and a sensation of threat. She tried to use her magnifying glass to burn a hole to escape, but could not, in her anxiety, find the direction of the sun.

Rooster-call awoke them. In the morning the children

discovered that the skinny boy Harold, from a house nearby, had been hired to feed the chickens. His thin cluck-clucking awoke them at daybreak, and they thought at first, with alarm, that Mrs Minchin had returned. Thomas persuaded Harold, on pain of Chinese burns, not to tell anyone of their return – he left a welt to show the seriousness of his threat – and so began their four days together, with only Harold and the blind woman knowing, and their whole world contracting to a curtain-drawn space.

Daytimes were easy: objects recovered their propriety, their habitual look, and the children played cards and read, or scavenged for eggs and tomatoes. Mrs O'Connor called over the fence and gave them a fruit cake. She had baked it herself, measuring the ingredients by mysterious means with her ugly mummified hands, and though the children ate it cautiously, plucking out the bitter green cherries with their fingernails and flicking them away, it served as reassuring evidence of her residual humanity. She left them alone, Mrs O'Connor did. The gift of the fruit cake was her only intervention.

In the afternoon the children shared the wicker chair, wedged closely together, and Thomas read to Lucy from his book about railways.

Neither could have said what transformation occurred at night, but it was detectable even on the surface of the skin. Their hands were gluey and their faces appeared waxen and old. Ned was unsettled and turned in tight circles, whimpering. Shadows hung everywhere, all of them elongated. The children lay again on their parents' bed, a little apart, and both were close to tears. Thomas moved his head and whispered into his sister's ear.

"If Mrs Minchin doesn't come back we'll go to Brazil."

"Brazil?" Lucy had never heard of it.

"There are jungles there, and gold. I'll find bucketsful of gold and we'll buy a passage to England and live there like swells. In a castle. Perhaps in Scotland."

Lucy was impressed by her brother's whispery vision. He sounded confident and sure.

"Like a princess?"

Thomas didn't even bother to reply. He was thinking, he said. Thinking and planning.

Lucy remembered the puzzling story of the Princess and the Pea. She lived in a castle, this princess, and everyone knew she was a princess because under fifty mattresses she could still feel the presence of a pea. Why was this so? Lucy was enchanted by the magical sensitivity of princesses, who were so acutely aware of the world they felt the tiniest impression.

"Or Africa," Thomas added. "There are diamonds in Africa."

"In bucketsful?"

"Oh, yes. Diamonds in bucketsful."

The grim night with its long shadows took on radiant possibilities.

Thomas had plans. Thomas would guide them.

So it was a surprise, later on, when Lucy was roused in the night — disturbed by a metaphysical shiver that awoke her — to find her brother walking in his sleep, apparently lost and bewildered. Thomas was naked and cradled his genitals in one hand; the other arm crossed his chest, reaching to the throat, as though feeling at the base of his neck for his pulse. It must have been near dawn, for the darkness was thinning, and Lucy could see his slender body, a pale human light, moving in slow motion in its otherworldly state, delicate, tentative, almost no longer her brother. She took the hand, which was shaking, away from his throat and as gently as she could, led him back to bed. He had the look of someone so nervous, so taut, that he would surely detect a hidden pea like a storybook princess. Lucy cradled her brother's head onto a pillow, careful not to look into his open eyes, and kissed him in the centre of the forehead, exactly in the centre, just as she had seen her living mother do.

7

IT WAS NOT A PHOTOGRAPH, BUT IT MIGHT HAVE BEEN, SINCE IT swam into Lucy's mind with the particular lucidity an image carries as it surfaces in its fluid, the lucidity of an entirely new vision, washed fresh into the world, wet with its image-birthing. It was of her mother as a child of seven or eight, standing in a pretty, flounced dress and a broad white hat, a hat which curved around her face like a materialising halo. This child looked directly ahead, but squinted slightly, as though she were peering into the future to meet her adult daughter's gaze, as though, in fact, the child knew it was possible that time might distort like this, might loop lacily and suddenly fold over. It was a canny image: the child seemed to know something of the future.

Behind the figure of Honoria Brady as a little girl was a mound of earth, perhaps fifteen feet high, a grass-covered hillock shaped like an old-fashioned beehive, and at the base of this mound there was a narrow tunnel. This structure was a handmade cave where ice, shipped in blocks from faraway places like Norway and Denmark, was stored for English country houses, so that the wealthy might have their chilled wine, their ice cream, their cold salmon and their ice packs. A suitable small hill was found, its interior hollowed out, and the ice stored there, settled in layers separated by straw. Kept in this manner ice could last up to eighteen months. Lucy knew about ice caves from her mother's story.

"Tell it again," she would say. "Tell the ice cave again."

And so her mother told it yet again and the swimming image of the little girl in the flounces and bonnet rose up, gained detail and gradually became fixed.

Honoria Brady was the only daughter of a widower, George, a young man not yet embittered, but dreaming of a New Beginning in Canada or Australia. The family lived in a small town on the edge of an estate in Nottinghamshire, where George worked as a lawyer's clerk and his son Neville attended the church school. Honoria stayed at home and though only seven, was expected to clean and tend the garden and learn cooking from an old woman who came each day to concoct some brown matter that she presented invariably as stew. It was a lonely time, and Honoria was a child given to escape and exploration. "Wayward" her father called her.

When she discovered the ice cave, on the property of the estate, Honoria was brave enough to enter. She walked into the tunnel, not needing to bend, but having no light saw only a kind of liquid glint, unidentifiable and veiled by shadows. Her hand pressed against something she thought at first was hot, so she withdrew it immediately. But the space was cool and damp, and the child felt safe and enclosed. Earth scent surrounded her and the air was watery, strange. When she returned with a candle the next day she discovered that what she had touched was ice, but she had never seen it in this abundant state before – a hidden mountain, tucked away and layered neatly with wet straw. She claimed this space as her own, and played there fantastic games with invisible friends. With a kitchen knife Honoria would chip away at the ice, and feed herself on its sparkly shards and slivers.

One day, perhaps inevitably, someone found her. The keeper

of the estate blundered through the tunnel, hunched over like a cripple, his giant shadow cast before him, to find the small child ensconced and perfectly at home. He seized her wrist and dragged her out. When he found her there again the following week, he marched her up to the large house for a reprimand from the mistress. (This is a part of the story Lucy disliked as a child, but enjoys now, as an adult, imagining her mother.)

In the large house Honoria met an ancient woman, a Lady Rosamund Leonowens, who peered at her through spectacles held on a fancy silver stick. She was stiff with black bombazine and frilled all over, and her head, Honoria said, was sharp and beaky, like a crow.

"Your punishment", the woman commanded, "is that you must read to me daily."

(Did Lady Leonowens really say this, or does Lucy require it to be so?) At this point Honoria confessed her illiteracy, and in a remarkable turn of events Lady Leonowens arranged for the child to have daily instruction in the alphabet, which she supervised herself. So it was that Honoria learned to read. Within a year, with flair and precocity, she was reading to the old woman. And when the family left for Australia, George Brady, who had known nothing at all of this strange transaction, was handed five guineas in a little purse, stained with tears, and an instruction that the child Honoria write regularly to her patron of her Colonial Adventures.

Lucy was six years old when she first heard this story. Even then, so young, it made her dizzy with pleasure. She had leaned into her mother's body, which was dusted with gardenia talcum powder and exceptionally sweet, and closed her eyes to see again the small girl in the cave, so brave and so clever, lighting up with her candle a whole mountain of ice.

Her mother bent to kiss her cheek.

"My Princess," she whispered.

8

FOR ARTHUR THE SILHOUETTE EXISTED SYMBOLICALLY, TO REMIND him of his honeymoon. To remind him that he had found and claimed Honoria. And not once, but twice. On the coach, and in Italy.

In their Florentine pensione it was clear to everyone they were newly wed: they had about them a nimbus of reciprocity and mutual regard and moved – as everyone noticed – as though in slow dance, each responding attentively to the shape of the other, to the subtle aesthetics and erotics of body configurations. Cynics were reminded that love is possible: here it was, incarnated. As the young man popped open an umbrella above his new wife, and she ducked beneath it, swiftly, in a pert concise arc, even their simplest movements were evidently beautiful.

The Pensione Rosa was full of English tourists, all of whom marvelled in chorus that anyone could have come so far. Australia signified a space so vast and remote that it was imaginable only in terms of exaggerated vacuity. The occasional black person or criminal, nightmarish flora and fauna, an empty dead centre where explorers wandered lost for a while and then vanished, heroically, into absolving thin air. Nothing much, really. Space. Immense space. Honoria and Arthur endured these descriptions with patient bemusement, but refused to feel pleased on being congratulated for their civilised manners and their English-language competence. On the whole, they decided, their fellow travellers were arrogant, hypochondriacal, rudely nationalistic, and excited only by the prospect of a game of bridge.

The exception, and there had to be one, was a Miss Harriet White, a character, said Honoria, straight out of a novel. She was a forty-two-year-old woman from south London who travelled as a companion to her aged aunt; and undaunted by her servile role to a somewhat demented relation, was lively, intelligent and habitually ironic. She and Honoria were instantaneous friends, and shared above all a love of reading. They exchanged novels and sat on the armoire together, their bodies inclined in the church-shape of serious conversation under a lamp of such flourish that it could only have been Italian. Arthur watched from a distance, aware of a kind of exclusion, but it was almost a week before he realised Miss White was a rival. Once they had come in from a stroll, having visited yet another generically picturesque church, and she rushed forward to greet them as they stood at the doorway. Even before Honoria had removed her overcoat and shaken her bonnet, Miss White had reached out to brush away raindrops that were clinging to her hair; this gesture was so intimate and possessive that Arthur felt himself clench with jealousy. From that moment he noticed everything with cheerless clarity: how singularly Miss White's attention was fixed on his wife, how she responded as he did, watching the nape of her neck, noticing how she habitually fiddled with her earrings, following her entire movement as she stooped to retie a shoe. Her smallest mannerisms arrested them both. Arthur thought of his heart as a coach, dragged in Honoria's direction.

The most painful moment was when his special gift was usurped. Honoria and Arthur had been window-shopping on the Ponte Vecchio when she had admired a pretty string of Venetian glass beads. Arthur resolved to return the next day and purchase the beads, but when he did they were gone, sold to somebody else, so that he bought instead another string – not quite so remarkable, but pearly and intricate and threaded with spirals of bronze. That evening, before Arthur could present his gift over dinner, Miss White intercepted them and presented her own. Honoria must have described to her friend the jewellery she admired, for there, in a black velvet case, lay what Arthur had sought. Honoria threw her arms around Harriet's neck and kissed her three times.

"How thoughtful," she exclaimed. "What a lovely surprise!"

He watched as Miss White fixed the clasp, brushing away strands of trailing hair. Honoria's hand strayed up to caress her throat.

"How thoughtful," she repeated.

She moved to a mirror and saw herself radiant.

"I'm afraid", Harriet added in a tone of mock seriousness, "they don't suit you at all. A dreadful vision!"

And then they both laughed, and kissed again.

Arthur's misery was acute. He felt he could not now present the lesser gift. Later he stored the pearly beads in the bottom of his luggage, his wounding secret. And he could not sleep for thinking of the women's faces, laughing in the mirror, and Miss White's slender fingers as they tended the clasp, and himself, dumb, appearing empty-handed.

It rained every day during the two weeks they spent in Florence. The stony streets shone and the façades of the buildings were slick with rain-light. Horse mess lay everywhere in fresh steaming piles; under carriage wheels it grew rank and dispersed in yellow streaks.

"Such a ripe, ripe city!" Honoria beamed.

Nothing disappointed her. Even the Arno, swollen with

debris, sullied with churning mud and the occasional drowned dog, she found delightful.

That Harriet was in love with Honoria was indisputable, but Arthur had to concede that she behaved with tact and restraint. In truth, he admired her. At the same time her presence made him insecure: she and Honoria had formed such a quick attachment and were intense in all their interactions. Their talk enlivened each other: it was some quality of concept or emotion, perhaps some texture of knowing, he found mysterious and felt he could not provide. Jealousy confused him and damaged his happiness.

One morning the women prepared to go off together: Miss White wanted to take Honoria to a little shop she claimed sold the finest papers and parchments in the world. When she noticed Arthur's discomfiture she invited him to accompany them, but, though miserable, he politely declined. Miss White extended the courtesy of drawing a map.

"We'll be here," she said, marking an X. "And shan't be more than two hours."

Arthur waited less than an hour before he set out to find them. The rain was dense and slanted. He pulled tighter his day-coat, and walked with untypical rapidity, clutching Miss White's map marked with its Honoria-location. Perhaps it was his hurry, or his anxiety, but Arthur quickly became lost. He entered a piazza to find that it was the one that he had left, and when he looked back over his shoulder, to the direction from which he had come, this too was unfamiliar. Stone walls loomed above him. The streets off the piazza were all similarly awash and indistinctive. Arthur fumbled to unfold Harriet's map but discovered it was smeared with moisture and all its details inky and irredeemable. Panic overtook him. Not that he would not find his way, but that he would not find *her*. His life seemed suddenly so very contingent: so much depended on the bright apparition of her face. He spun around, feeling helpless, then simply fled, choosing a street at random and hurtling down it. He doubled back, and zigzagged and became hopelessly confounded. When Arthur finally paused and leaned against a stone wall, his heart was racing. (Mustn't cry, he thought, a grown man, a foreigner, on the streets of Florence.) The rain had stopped but Arthur did not seem to notice. He set off again, a child-sob ballooning in his chest.

When she appeared before him he was almost unsure, but yes, the floral gown beneath the maroon-coloured overcoat, the precise tilt of her bonnet, her profile within it. Honoria was alone, staring into a shop window some distance ahead, and as Arthur rushed forwards and startled her, she immediately smiled. *Annunciation*, he thought. *Annunciation: her face.* All over Italy he had seen images in which the passage of spirit was rendered in a faint dotted line, a love-corridor, a dedication. Something in these particular images had moved him: the affirmation of imperceptible connection.

"Look at this," said Honoria, as she directed his gaze through a window, which was not in fact a shop but a craftsman's workplace. A pretty woman sat in the window, staring to one side, and in the dim recess behind her an old man bent at a wooden desk, cutting out her profile in thin black paper. He worked with tiny implements and with extreme concentration, and not from a sketch but from the purposeful acuity of his vision.

"Harriet is off seeking a carriage," Honoria said distractedly.

She had no idea, he realised, of his watery dissolution, his panic in installments, or his recovery in her presence.

"So clever," she murmured.

He peered then, with care, and saw in the old man's antique fastidious labour some measure of his own pernickety devotion.

Honoria was persuaded to have her profile cut. When, ten

minutes later, Harriet White passed by, looking a little troubled and glancing all around her, Arthur rushed into the street to guide her in, and they sat quietly together, watching their beloved emerge, painstakingly, as a silhouette in black paper. Against the bright window Honoria appeared as a figure cut into pure light.

"It's rather morbid," declared Harriet. "I don't like it at all. Like mourning brooches. Like death."

But Arthur rejoiced. This token. This sign.

9

IN THE DARKNESS LUCY AWOKE WITH A START, AND CALLED OUT "MA!"

And it was her brother, Thomas, who roused to tend her. He stretched out his hand, groping like a blind person, like the Egyptian Mrs O'Connor, and found and stroked her cheek.

"There's someone out there, at the window," Lucy complained.

She sounded so little, like an infant of two or three. Fright had reversed her.

Thomas said: "No, go back to sleep."

"But there is. There is." (She whined, she sobbed.)

So he rose, lit a candle, and saw himself reflected in the glass window pane, a boy-genie, quaking. His face was the colour of saffron, and in the strange zone of night glass he seemed to waver and shift, his body composed of coloured smoke. He could see his chest, his nipples, his startled-looking eyes.

"It's the wattle tree, I think. A branch is scraping at the window."

Lucy was reassured. He heard her turn over behind him, sigh, and re-settle.

Thomas remained standing before the window. This impersonation of himself was more fearsome than his father's face appearing on the hallway mirror. The dark around him was welling, as though it would swallow and cover him. *Darkness in bucketsful.* Yet the force of his own double fixed him still, and this ordinary sight, compelled by so ordinary a reflective phenomena, was the hypnotic confirmation of a solitude that he would carry throughout his life, unassuaged by adulthood or success or lovers in his bed, untempered by rational or sensible assessment. Part of him would always be this insubstantial and isolated boy, fictitious, yellow, paralleled by alienation, barely there on the glass in the middle of the night.

"I'm cold," Lucy whimpered softly.

Thomas was sweating, aflame.

IO

WHAT COUNTRY HAD THEY COME TO, WITH SUCH ENORMOUS SKY?

Honoria had been seasick for much of the journey and had imagined the worst. With a damp rag over her eyes and tears in her heart, with the harrowing creak of their wooden vessel straining against the weight of the sea, the air dense with fish-stink and brine and the shouts of labouring men, her father and brother on the deck somewhere, her whole mood one of abandonment, Honoria fabricated an Australia that was the culmination of ill-omen. She imagined it grey, contained, fetid and dank. She imagined their ship churning its way towards some nauseating disaster. In the swoon of such unhappiness it was not possible to imagine otherwise.

There had been one or two periods of brief respite, when she had left her hammock and seen the sky. Once it was so windless the ship had simply stopped: it bobbed in one place, poised and placid, and Honoria and Neville had raced around the deck whooping with pleasure. Fat sea birds settled to watch them play, their red eyes curious. For three days there existed a splendid calm; the sky was blank and benevolent; the sun shone brightly. But when the ship resumed its churning Honoria resumed her illness; she had never been so miserable.

In the hammock in the women's section the ladies fussed at first, but soon grew tired of this child who was always poorly and prostrate. One, an Irish girl, persisted in care; Nell bent over Honoria, broad-faced and loving, her lilting voice the gentle waves it was possible to be buoyed on; and when the child vomited salt meat, she alone stayed to clean her, and when the child woke in the night, she embraced and comforted her; so that her bending over became at length the entire shape of the ship, and the only thing, this shape, Honoria will remember of the journey. In the future, in a sleepless moment, after the birth of her first baby, Honoria will recall uncannily the taste of Jamaica ginger in her mouth; and in her dreamy state recall also the curve around her loneliness that was broad-faced Nell. It was both a composite and an indefinite recollection: a taste, a name, a durable unfolding. And it allowed Honoria to believe she had not spent her own life motherless, but had been multiply mothered. A number of women had found and held her, all of them ship-shaped. For now, however, there is this extenuated abjection and these long blindfolded days, and more than anything Honoria knows the murmur of the ocean; she hears it swell and sound when everyone else is asleep; it is her most loyal, most consistent, familiar. Sometimes there are whispered messages or hazy half-stories. And sometimes there is nothing: mere tedious repetition. Honoria's voice is strangulated, as if it issues from a cave, so Nell sings and speaks and uses voice enough for both of them; and they coexist in this pathetic affectionate union, in the belly of the wooden ship, rocked and rolled together.

Neville had to breach the women's section to drag Honoria from her hammock to see it – their New Beginning country. The harbour was dazzling. The children made Chinese eyes against the Australian glare. Honoria could hardly believe that the world was after all so large and the sky so bright an immensity; she had been too long confined. She clung to her brother and watched the new world wobble and grow closer

– the opal water, the prismatic light, the sight of a large ship-ping dock and its ramshackle buildings, all brown and noisy, sliding unevenly to greet them. It was a mythic arrival. Honoria felt Nell shift position to stand behind her, and finger-tips move in her unbound hair. She felt her brother's hand-clasp and her own miraculous light-heartedness. Something floated inside her; it was the New Beginning, perhaps, or just the sudden heaven – after so much illness – of solid landfall.

The boarding house they moved into was shabby but clean. The landlady smelled of gin and entertained portly gentlemen with large moustaches. In the smallish parlour there was a pianola, warped by damp, chintz furniture featuring a pattern of rusty autumn leaves, a set of four prints displaying views of Windsor Castle, as well as a spoilt, yappy lapdog that detested children. George Brady complained – he was already learning the expatriate modes of bitterness – the heat, the foreignness, the less-than-expected remuneration, all sorts of vague subtractions he perceived or imagined – but his children pros-pered. In their unbitter child-hearts even the boarding house was an adventure. The children spied on their landlady undressing, tilted her castles, taunted her stupid dog, and roamed the Sydney streets in which everything, even voices, were incalculably novel and full of surprise. The blindness Honoria had been folded into during the torturous voyage unfolded like a fan to show a concertina of spectacles. And when she stood on the dock, watching the large slow ships, with their pale sails fluttering, she found it difficult to remem-ber her own captive time. Life had started with that view of the harbour, its sunlit revelation.

II

ON THE THIRD DAY THE CHILDREN LOOKED AT THEIR PARENTS'
belongings. It was Thomas's idea: he started opening drawers
in a casual, almost desultory manner, but then he found
himself peering into them, and rummaging about. He looked
guilty, Lucy thought. But soon enough, she joined him.

Their parents both seemed to have possessed large quantities of under-garments, and endless drawers filled with layers
and layers of day-clothes. There were shirts, blouses, scarves,
jackets and handkerchiefs. Both had boxes of hats, some of
which were archaic and these days unfashionable, and among
the hatboxes Thomas found one which contained odds and
ends of bric-a-brac he realised must have belonged to his father:
a child's bamboo flute, stamped with the design of a red
dragon, a tiny gondola, carved in onyx, a grubby set of playing cards, of which certain numbers were missing, a charm of
some sort (a cross-legged oriental man, corpulent and smiling), a little notebook with jottings in a Chinese script, and a
few small-denomination coins, apparently Italian. The modest
specificity of these objects moved Thomas to tears; he had a
sense, for the first time, of his father as a boy. He found
himself touching each object in turn, as though touch alone
would furnish the quality of reverence that might break open
and expose their secret history. The Italian objects were all

infrangibly enigmatic; but he knew a little of his father's Chinese boyhood, and imagined him, perhaps ludicrously, in a pointy hat and baggy pyjamas, sitting in a scene rather like that on a willow-pattern plate – that magical pagoda, those cauliflower trees, that semicircular bridge – and playing this very flute. When Lucy reached for it he slapped her, not sure what instinct he enacted.

Both children moved around their parents' room avoiding the mirror: it might somehow incriminate them. From her mother's dressing table Lucy took up an inlaid box, of mother-of-pearl, and opened it on the bed. She spread before her an assortment of trinkets and jewellery: rings, bracelets, a particularly lovely string of beads, but these were items she had seen and even touched before, in other more clandestine and naughty investigations. Nevertheless death had somehow condensed their meaning: they marked the body gone. These were objects that had hung from her mother's thin bony wrists, that had encircled her fingers, that in characteristic and girlish gestures she had fiddled with and fondled as she thoughtfully spoke; and these beads of cold glass had rested in that slight blue concavity of the neck where the pulse, *her pulse*, had been visibly detectable. Lucy could barely bring herself to touch them. She felt as if there were knots tied in her chest. She scooped everything together in a tangled mess, and heaped it back into the inlaid box. (Mustn't cry, she thought, with Thomas already like that, so tearful and girlie.)

It was the wardrobe, however, that disturbed her resolve. For when Lucy opened the door she was overcome with a posthumous scent of gardenia, and at that moment, saturated with a who-knows-what betokening, stirred by something so imprecise it was not even a memory, but the latent and restless breeze of a memory, she too became tearful. She slumped into the perfumed cavity, her limbs drawn up, her face buried in the hanging folds of her mother's dresses, winding sheets now, limp and deadly, and untied all the knots she had been tying to hold herself together. So Thomas wept for the specific, for the tangible object, the flute and the whistle and the missing breath that would animate them, and Lucy for a vague vibration in the air, for the dusty sweetness that lingered when it should have been absent. It shocked them both, these tears so late in the peace. Thomas found handkerchiefs monogrammed "A", and the children wiped their faces and blew their noses. Then they were quiet for a long, long time. The room was solemn, shadowy and still. Wattle-filtered light gave everything an effaced appearance.

The next day Lucy discovered her mother's objects. Like her father's they were encrypted in secret histories. At the bottom of the wardrobe, pushed back, was a further hatbox, and in this one, no different from the others, rested a few hidden-away mother-things.

A wedding card, stamped with the paw of an animal.

A second string of Italian beads, even more lovely.

A diaphanous scarf, with beadwork in its fringes.

A copy of *Jane Eyre*, with passages underlined.

A bundle of letters, on writing paper textured like the surface of the ocean, from someone called Harriet.

A list of names: Eleanor, Harriet, Lucy, Rosamund. (Lucy underlined.)

A mourning brooch, containing a single curl of blonde hair.

A purse of coins, apparently Italian, of small denominations.

A satin ribbon, leaf green, with "I adore you" written along it in precise black ink. (This neatly rolled.)

At first the appearance of her own name was like a mystical sign: it placed *Lucy* like a code-breaker in a system of secrets. Yet it was also, Lucy realised, estranged and useless. The hatbox was a little amnesiac circle: everything was lost and without association. Nothing summoned her mother's face. Nothing was intelligible. Lucy will spend the rest of her life looking intently at faces. She becomes, at this very moment, one whose mission it is to unconceal. This is the moment, aged eight, Lucy becomes a photographer. And every photographic ambition will turn on the summoning of a face and the retrieval of what is languishing just beyond vision.

Years later, in the middle of the night, in a pleat in time, Lucy wakes to find herself whispering the words: mother-of-pearl. She remembers the jewellery box and the scented wardrobe. She remembers the leaf-green ribbon and the bundle of letters. It occurs to her then that this is the light, the diffuse glimmering light, she has seen inherent in wet collodion and silver-nitrate photographic prints. The light of mother-of-pearl. It is the light one sees, half-awake, in grey early morning. It is the light that glances off faces, glimpsed in the act of love-making. It is the light of memory, and of the earliest petals of gardenia. It is the blurred aura, perhaps, between concealment and unconcealment.

12

IN THE NOVEL *JANE EYRE* A TREE IS CLEFT BY LIGHTNING. THE GODDESS
Nature is so responsive to the movements of lovers that she
sends prophesying icons to confirm the progress of their
romance.

"I know it's preposterous," Honoria said. "But isn't it also
wonderful?"

She told this episode with such fervour that Arthur was
enchanted. She lay in his arms and her curly hair brushed at
his face. He was aware of her soft cheek, and the rise of her
voice. This ocean they rode on, this amatory cradle, he imagined was their own natural authentification.

Even then, especially then, he had wanted to tell his own story,
but for some reason could not. His *lightning* story.

How old had he been: six? His father was working in the
centre, in Wuhan, and he and his mother were travelling by
ox cart back to Hangkow, on the coast. It was in the middle of
the summer, and he remembers the din of crickets issuing
from the banyan and the powdery dust billowing upwards in
high clouds behind them. The taste of salt lumps and green tea
that his mother fed him. The sunburn upon which she had
rubbed some indigenous ointment, so that his European skin
was a glossy tangerine. A tiny man in a pointy hat squatted at

the front of the cart, and Arthur sat behind with his mother beneath a wax paper umbrella, its small shade rocking and jerking around them. Everywhere people stood in doorways to stare. Sometimes children his own age jogged beside the cart, reaching up with pale hands, and shouting: "Devil! Devil!"

"Just ignore them," said his mother.

But Arthur never could. He shouted back and joked in their own language — which his mother could not understand — and was annoyed that they teased him, calling him a foreign devil, because he was English and sunburned and rode beneath an umbrella and in a woman's guarded embrace.

At some point on their journey they were on a stretch of lonely road. The wind fell suddenly to nothing and the sky coloured deep purple. Arthur sensed his mother's anxiety in the fluttering of her fan, and when he looked at her face — he sees it even now — he saw that her loose hair was standing on end, an affrighted halo, and that her features were tightened and seized with fear. His scalp was prickling and he could feel his own hair uprisen, neat as new rice. Thunder filled the air above them, sharp, aslant lightning appeared in the sky, and when their cart driver leapt up and ran away down the road, his mother began to chant:

"The Lord is my shepherd; I shall not want,
He maketh me to lie down in green pastures;
He leadeth me beside the still waters.
He restoreth my soul . . ."

Arthur was decisive. He seized his mother's wrist and they ran together, rather stumblingly, rather blindly, into a field of dry grass. He does not really know exactly what occurred — everywhere was illuminated, mauve and alive with electricity — except that some force burnt his feet and toppled him over, and when he woke he was on his back, looking up at the sky. His entire body ached, and his sunburn felt so painful he thought perhaps he had been burned alive. Soft rain spattered and bathed his face. He felt alert and stimulated. The sky was lovely, like crystal, with the calm and translucence of the departed storm. A single bird, a crane, slid slowly overhead.

When Arthur turned his head to look for his mother, she was lying at a short distance, her eyes closed, the hem of her long skirt slightly smouldering, and at first, in dread and ignorance, he thought that she was dead. But she stirred, and began to cry. Arthur put his arm around her, and brushed rain from her face. She was like a little girl. When she recovered her adulthood she stood, adjusted her bonnet and tugged at her bodice, as though she were preening for a Sunday outing, and then looked around for her umbrella and fan. The umbrella's fabric had burnt away, so that it was just a radial structure of sticks, but the fan had been left behind in the ox cart, and was sodden but unspoiled. Arthur remembers that, in her absentmindedness, his mother took up the umbrella, useless though it now was, and brought it with them.

The ox was dead. Its large eyes were wide open and rolled back into white balls. The driver was gone. They stayed together, mother and son, in the stalled ox cart, the huge carcass yoked in a stinking death, and together they chanted:

"Yea, though I walk through the valley of the shadow of Death,
I will fear no evil, for Thou art with me.
Thy rod and Thy staff they comfort me . . ."

The sun returned. Flies began to gather in the nostrils and eyes of the ox. Arthur and his mother lay beneath the ox cart for shade, fanned each other's skin, and waited to be found. When another cart arrived, driven by a surprised old man, it was Arthur's task — though by then he was barely sensible — to explain what had happened, and to bargain payment for their ride. And still his mother chanted; and still she clutched her umbrella and fluttered her chrysanthemum fan.

13

HE HAD WANTED FOR YEARS TO TELL HER, BUT NOW IT WAS TOO
late. In his maddened state of grief, in the dark, dark shadow
of the valley of death, Arthur itemised all that he had not said,
all that he had not given, all his repressed or stammering or
incomplete endearments, all the secrets still locked away in his
coach-carriage heart. He had wanted to tell Honoria about
his mother. He had wanted to tell her how she appeared.

That she had risen from fiery death, brushed herself down,
adjusted her bonnet, tidied up, and then taken and held aloft
a burnt-out umbrella. And Arthur had looked up and seen
encircling his mother's head a radial structure of sticks, a
Florentine halo, through which, in dazzling mauve, shone
spokes of storm-swept sky.

14

THE TREES AT THE WINDOW SHIVERED, JUST AS SHE SHIVERED WITH
the delectable cool of his touch. The way he unpinned her
hair and spread it open with his fingertips. The initial stroke
of his open hand against her breast.

In the first two years of their marriage Honoria Strange had
unlearned and relearned her body, and now, at twenty, it
seemed untutored again. Yet she faced herself naked in the
mirror and experienced her own existence as complete self-
possession. Her breasts had inflated to bulbs and her belly was
a globe; an indigo filament ran from her navel to her pubic
hair, and veins she did not know existed were now apparent
across her chest. She examined herself as an artist might: finding the immanent aesthetic. The curves that composed her.
The tissue artfully distended. The venerable imperfections and
discolourations that graded her body more solidly. Honoria
felt at once real and achieved. If she doubted her future body
at all it was because she did not wish the shivering to cease.

The pregnancy had been without incident or mishap, and
now Mrs Minchin had arrived, for the last weeks before the
birth. At first Honoria was taken aback to see the woman's
face: it bore a wine-dark pigmentation across most of the left
side, and blemished an otherwise handsome woman. In an
episode of superstition she had asked Arthur whether she

might now deliver a baby with a birthmark, and he told her it was a foolish and unbecoming supposition. Honoria was ashamed; for years later she thought of it and blushed at her youthful ignorance. (Nevertheless — and she could tell no-one — she had a recurrent nightmare in which she nursed a baby whose too-tiny face was disfigured by red shadow.)

As her time approached Honoria Strange grew flagrantly lazy. She lay about the house, rather dishevelled, in a thin linen nightgown studded with girlish pink bows, and gradually befriended the wine-dark Molly Minchin. When they grew to know each other Honoria discovered that this woman was exceptional: she knew of happenings both natural and supernatural, she performed skills both ordinary and wonderfully extraordinary — midwifery, divination, communication with spirits — and had travelled to far lands and exotic locations.

Molly had been one of a family of six children raised in Southern India, where she had grown boldly accustomed to her own conspicuousness. Sometimes people retreated, even fled, when they saw her face; sometimes she was garlanded with marigolds and jasmine and touched by the brown fingers of reverent strangers. In both cases the little memsahib was always stared at. She grew to know her own visibility and importance in the world; she was confident and sure in a way that her two younger sisters, both pretty and blonde-haired, would never experience. As a child, Molly explained, she reasoned that since the god Krishna was blue, why shouldn't she be whitish from the neck down and rose-coloured on top? Frederick Minchin, a sea captain, saw at once the complex nature of Molly's specificity, not just that she was bi-coloured, but in many ways exemplary. Their marriage was spent in the Far East, on the ocean, sexually vigorous and wholly companionable, until Frederick was one night washed into the darkness by a freak storm off the island of Java. A widow at thirty-five, Molly had suffered four miscarriages during their life together: her main regret, she said, was the washing-away of the children.

Molly Minchin told Honoria Strange a series of fabulous tales — of a Dutch balloonist who floated above Madras in a gondola-shaped basket, only to fall out, spectacularly, when he leaned to catch a letter he had dropped; of a woman named Minnie who married a Musilman in Lucknow and was so beloved of her husband that he ordered the sacrifice of white peacocks on the occasion of her death; of a fierce goddess who wore human skulls around her neck as adornment, and was depicted in temples with her tongue out, dripping blood; of elephant madness and wild lion hunts, of palaces and palanquins, of vast Persian monuments. The little wooden house in Melbourne filled with unreal treasures and eastern exaggerations. Molly supplied the enlarged imaginary to match Honoria's pregnant expansiveness. In return Honoria Strange told the widow Molly Minchin the entire plot, in detail, of the novel *Jane Eyre*.

Honoria was intuitively convinced she would deliver a girl, and wrote out a series of names on a piece of paper. Molly underlined Lucy, so *Lucy* it was, and they were both surprised when a boy arrived, yowling and angry, its face oriental, to contest their presumption. Arthur was overjoyed: he named the baby Thomas in honour of his paternal grandfather, whose sermons, full of excitable and authoritarian righteousness, he still clearly recalled.

This is what Honoria remembers: Molly examined the body of the baby and found it was without birthmark or distinguishing sign. So with charcoal she drew a round flaw on the right side of Thomas's cheek: this was necessary, Molly said, to protect the unmarked child from the evil eye that sees and destroys what is too pure and too beautiful. Honoria thought the charcoal mark looked like a burn, as though the baby's skin had been scorched with a magnifying glass. When Lucy was born, two years later, she carried a strawberry birthmark on the left side of her chest: Molly said this was perfect. The girl-child must be physically marked on the left, and her relation to the forces of benevolence and malevolence was vouched safe and secure. Honoria was relieved that this face, this at-last-come-daughter, was not besmirched as her son had been. When she rose at night to feed, her daughter's face was the beckoning lamp she moved through darkness to embrace. A taste in her own mouth, mysteriously, of Jamaican ginger. A vague envisioning. The envelope of a breathing space from elsewhere and long ago.

She remembers, too, that on the joyous birth day of her daughter, Arthur gave her a string of beads he had saved for years from the time of their honeymoon in Florence. She was surprised at this little ordination from the past. They were lovely beads, pearly and intricate and threaded with glinting spirals of bronze. When he placed them at her neck, fumbling with the clasp, the cold of the glass made her suddenly shiver. How she loved his hands there, at the nape of her neck, and the sexual intimation of so delicate, so fluttering, a touch.

15

WHAT WAS IT LIKE, LUCY WONDERED, TO BE MRS O'CONNOR? WHAT must it mean to live alone, in continuous black, where the whole world is adjusted to an idiom of anxiety, to the keen mnemonic placement of heavy objects, to the intractable logic of shapes and surfaces, to a strict attunement to decipherable and indecipherable sound? And where, worst of all, what is lost is the engendering image of the face. As a child she imagined it more simply: an unawakening.

"It's really not that bad," declared Mrs O'Connor. "I have my cooking and my piano. I have my knitting. I have my friends who stop and chat, and once a week someone from the church comes over to read. It's far too easy", she added, "to overestimate seeing."

She was seated − enthroned, it seemed − in a lozenge of sunlight. She was preserved in a shape she could never know.

Mrs O'Connor felt the rim of a cup as she guided her teapot spout forward to pour.

"What I love", she added, "is very loud birds. We have so many in this country, filling the sky."

After this Lucy heard loud birds singing all week. A single sentence had reorganised the presences of the world. A single sentence. Just one.

Lucy visited Mrs O'Connor when she was bored with

Thomas and could no longer bear the stupefying misery of their house. The old woman welcomed her company and fed her cupcakes and tea; she patted Ned, who wagged his tail and nuzzled warmly at her lap. At length, on sufferance, Lucy consented to be touched. Mrs O'Connor drew near and ran her fingers slowly across Lucy's features, beginning with the forehead, feeling gently the cavities of the eyes with her thumbs, noting the shape of the nose, the outline of the lips, the contour and curve and declension of the chin, and assessing over all the girl-presence before her.

"Your face is a triangle," she said. "And you have very soft skin. I was spotty when I was a young woman and could see. Am I spotty now?"

"Yes, very spotty."

Lucy, without hesitating, had told the truth.

Mrs O'Connor laughed: they liked each other.

The old woman wore circular black spectacles, thick as ale-bottle ends, so that her blindness was private and could not be gazed on. Her house was rather dirty – with spidery corners and drifting fluff – but in other ways it was like the house of a sighted person: there were the usual decorations, white place mats, china ornaments, a line of ugly toby jugs; and there were prints on the wall – one of a fox hunt (the men convention-ally erect, the hounds poised and alert and snobbishly sniffing the air), and another of a vase of mixed flowers settled behind a bowl of assorted fruits (all tinted rather luridly to celebrate the doubled variety). Lucy stared at these prints and reflected that not seeing them was no terrible deprivation: some things should be seen – faces in particular – some things perhaps could be consigned, without loss, to blindness. She had the primitive intuition of an order of imagery, a personal scheme in which one might select and abolish, and in which clear-sightedness was committed to merit and exultation. Lucy closed her eyes to enter Mrs O'Connor's true house. She stretched out her arms against the world destroyed and was surprised that there was no completely obliterating black, but penumbral gradations and hazy rays. She opened, then closed her eyes, opened again, closed again. Some fundamental mystery inhered in the blinking of worlds: iris in, iris out.

Sometimes they played a game of chess together. Mrs O'Connor always won. She remembered the board with such precision that interruptions did not distract her and conversation did not trouble the visionary chessboard in her head. Lucy watched her long spindly fingers – what Thomas called, with a puckered look, her Mummy hands – reach carefully towards the board, locate a chess piece, and then feel and record its minute carved features. She was a decisive player, but acted slowly. Lucy told her about Fen and the glittering dress, about her trembling grandfather, James, who also played chess, and about the Chinese cousins. Mrs O'Connor told Lucy about her grown-up twin daughters, Flora and Dora, who now lived far away, in the West, and about how in dreams she would see herself flying over the desert to meet them. She was sighted in dreams, although she saw only what she had seen before she was blind, so that Flora and Dora remained eternally infant, two or three years old, and the location of her dreams was always her last visible landscape. "But the desert light", she said, "is absolutely scintillating."

"Scintillating?" Lucy had never heard the word before.

"All blinking and bright. Even the stones seem to shine."

Lucy pondered her knowledge: that asleep this woman saw. And not just anything, but the *scintillating* desert. When she told Thomas that afternoon he did not believe a word.

But Thomas too thought about it, many years later. Is it possible to summon as an after-image on the surface of the retina some image-memory that has lain, pristine and packed away, unglimpsed since early adulthood? As an old man he wants to will this, to dream resurrections, as blind Mrs O'Connor did. To recover his dead sister's face, drifting over the surface of a desert.

16

MARRIAGE IS AN OBTUSE AND STUBBORN STATE. SOMETIMES COUPLES live in the most intimate and consistent proximity, day after day, year after year, but know almost nothing significant of each other. A catalogue of shared experiences is dissolved in clouds of unknowing; there are vast selves undiscovered, and vast secret lonelinesses.

Honoria and Arthur loved but did not know each other. In a stiff white collar, gabardine suit and new leather shoes, Arthur had married a woman dressed in a fountain of ivory gauze, whom he had met six months earlier, accidentally, as it were, climbing from an overturned coach with a kitten. It was fated, he thought, but it was also precarious. From the beginning he feared the possibility of annulment, that he would bore or infuriate her, that she would discover in him a vacancy, that she would leave, or die. His marriage was characterised by a quality of amorous panic.

Less than a year after their wedding Arthur discovered among Honoria's possessions a leaf-green ribbon on which was printed, in an exceptionally neat hand, the single sentence, "I adore you". He was consumed by misery, believing not that Honoria was unfaithful, but that she had a previous lover. Yet although the idea shaded every encounter and conversation, he was never able to ask her to confirm or deny. Something

– it may simply have been the banality of his own humiliation – inhibited Arthur; he lived the years of his marriage with this object dangling, a parodic Damocles' sword, soft and prettily fluttering, above all the presents he lived in and the futures he projected. Then there was all that he was not able to tell – the miracle-of-the-lightning, the delirious hunt in Florence, the fact that he missed, excessively, his work as a coach driver (all that jolting motion, the mutable fleeing world, the small children waving and leaping and running dangerously alongside, the wind, the horses, the stewed tea in cooling flasks). His appointment at the bank had been a kind of spiritual death.

And then, more secretly, there was his errant body. On his ninth birthday, his first in Australia, Arthur looked at his body and saw that it was covered in a rash. He was coloured bright crimson, from top to toe, marked out in marbled flushes and crepey textures. His father suffered awful and unnecessary fears on his behalf. They consulted the most expensive physician in Sydney – a Doctor Roland, a man of hairy nostrils, hawk nose, a fat mole on his left eyelid – how clearly Arthur remembers the details of his face – but for all these caricaturing features, a man astute and gentle. Dr Roland examined the boy carefully, asked many and various impertinent questions, and then pronounced him to be suffering a mental condition. The trauma of grief, he said, had a symbolic birthday-association. Moreover the new country, the upheaval, the general upset of re-establishment . . . He peered over his spectacles with a mildly tut-tutting air, implying the redundancy of fuss or worry. James was dumbfounded, but agreed to no medication, and within a week the rash had disappeared. It returned again on Arthur's tenth birthday, and on the eleventh and twelfth. On the thirteenth it was faint, and by the fourteenth this mysterious and exhibitionist unhappiness that wrote itself on skin, radiant as a sin, was at last exhausted. Arthur was never able to tell his wife Honoria. How could he have explained this beacon body, that signalled to the world his boyhood guilt and distress? Even as a man he found himself scrutinising his skin each birthday, peering under his arms, lifting his scrotum, examining his back — twisted around, in the bedroom mirror — troubled yearly by the threat of recurrence or discovery. He had a nightmare, retained from nine years old, in which his body permanently changed colour. This handsome adult, Arthur Strange, carried a vision of himself — derived from childhood memories of Chinese mosaics in which chubby-faced demons, extraordinarily ugly, tumbled out-of-control in dragon-swirling clouds — a vision in which he saw himself as a monster, in garish magenta.

From the beginning Honoria had wanted Arthur to talk more about himself, but he never did. She suspected that her coach-driver lover was not as one-tracked as he appeared, but suffered the usual trackless ambiguities and occasional upheavals. In any case he would sometimes begin to say something, and then halt, and close off, locking away his secrets in some clandestine compartment. Her head was full of all the whispering, only just unintelligible, he might one day have told her.

What Honoria could not tell Arthur was that the world, since Italy, had been terribly disappointing. Her reading had established great expectations: books led her to believe that adventure was everywhere to be had, that catastrophes, coincidences and conjugal excitations abounded, that lives were melodramatically enhanced and symbolically under-written. After their metaphoric beginning — this man sliding on his belly into her carriage, the whole coach stalled to allow the generation of romance — their lives had become rather literal and prosaic. Honoria stayed at home, in the wooden cottage, minding the two children, while Arthur worked at the bank. They could afford no servants, travel or entertainment: the excursion to Italy seemed now a kind of novelistic conclusion. (In Honoria's imagination she is fixed in a pony-trap, looking backwards at an ever-receding Florentine duomo. Ribbons from her bonnet strike softly at her rain-damp face.)

In the coach she had been another Jane Eyre, full of self-righteous destiny and bound-for-glory; but now she thought, with ridiculous intensity, of the locked-away madwoman. She was assailed by an indistinct sense of imprisonment and remembered almost daily the character who chose immolation. How could she tell Arthur that he had confined and immobilised her?

Neither could Honoria tell Arthur about the force of her desire. He was a modest man, rather embarrassed by his body – she had once seen him scrutinise it with an almost trance-like engagement – but her sense of arousal and interest seemed more or less perpetual. She would have made love every night because she was always ready; and she knew too that there is a secret history of marriage, its true, ineffable, voluptuous history, which consists solely in the unrecordable reverberations of embrace. Arthur did not know that he was handsome, or that his body was beautiful. When they fell apart, panting, she would look across at him and see that his sweat-soaked chest was rising and rosy. That he was ashine. That he was her beacon.

17

SHE TURNED THE KEY IN THE DOOR AND KNEW THAT SOMETHING WAS wrong.

Mrs Minchin returned to the house to discover the children ensconced and mutinous as ever. Lucy was delinquent, Thomas sullen. She was at a loss to know how she might win them over. Even the gentle dog, Ned, now growled when she approached.

Her own grief had deposited her on a kind of ghost ship, somewhere. She felt she was invisibly drifting, unmoored, directionless, caught up in a blue foggy vision in which all shapes were unreliable, and her own existence a rumour. She felt herself to be without will or substance; she was in no state to nurture someone else's children. After her initial busyness had subsided, there was just blank mourning, and desolation.

It would be another eleven years before she saw Lucy again, but then they would love each other, and would at last confide.

For now, however, Molly Minchin faced the thankless task of managing two unhappy orphans until their uncle arrived. The days were long and tedious. The children refused to go to school and spent their time in the laneway or behind the hen-house, playing with the skinny boy, Harold, disappearing for hours, getting up to mischief and God-only-knows. Once she discovered them lighting fires with a magnifying glass, and realised with a pang of mingled anger and sadness that Lucy had for some time been systematically destroying her clothes. She punished the child, who would not apologise, by locking her away in the cupboard-sized pantry, but Lucy became so hysterically distraught, banging with her fists at the splintery door, screeching like a harpy, that Thomas, without permission, intervened to release her. The girl flew in a rage from the pantry, shouting "Ugly! Ugly!", before, aghast at her own infuriated cruelty, she burst into tears and ran sobbing from the room. After that the widow-midwife did not even try to befriend them: the children hated her.

Molly Minchin, whose birthmark granted her, for better or worse, an irresistible visibility, found companionship at last with Mrs O'Connor for whom, in the formal democracy of blindness, her face was merely another felt shape. The old woman touched her tenderly, and praised the formation of her nose; her hands, thought Molly, were a benediction. She was reminded of certain holy men of her Indian childhood: this aura of release and self-sufficiency. Only to Mrs O'Connor could she speak of her recent past, of her love for Honoria Strange and the botched-up birthing, of the disfigured baby and the bucketful of blood that soaked through the bed-sheets and spread on to the floor. She told of her guilt about Arthur; how she had guessed his intention, but had not known how to save him; how she had discovered him – his eyes fixed open, his mouth afroth, his body petrified in a belly-ache shape and looking wretchedly reduced – and how, for the second time, she had tidied up death. Finally she told Mrs O'Connor about her peculiar state, that she felt she was drifting, blown by a heavy sigh. The old woman said nothing, but held her hands. She was silent for a long time; perhaps she had fallen asleep. And then Mrs O'Connor unexpectedly stirred.

"Now, now," she said tenderly. "Now, now; now, now."

Two months after the scene at the pantry Uncle Neville arrived. The children knew of him only as a name, and were confused by how little he resembled their mother. This man might have been anyone, masquerading as an uncle. He was short and dark, his face slightly toadlike and his body pot-bellied, and he was dressed in soiled-looking flannel and a drooping hat. He carried an anomalously elegant walking cane, ringed with beaten silver, and topped by a carved ivory elephant. A man with little experience of children, he spoke to them remotely, as though he was addressing a large audience, of his dear-departed sister, and their duty to love one another, of the road ahead, which was England, of New Beginnings and Destiny Abroad. He dabbed at rheumy eyes with a filthy handkerchief.

Thomas was more than ever resolute in his plan to abscond to Brazil: "This man is a fool," he whispered to his sister, "and not to be trusted."

"And he stinks," Lucy added, clasping her wrinkled nose.

For his part, Neville Brady was also confused. He was a man so habitually dishonest that he once sent a stolen portrait of a soldier – upright, handsome, with a handlebar moustache and an honest gaze – to his dying father, the purloined image of a man masquerading as a son. George Brady was by then so twisted to his guts by lifelong bitterness he was not particularly consoled by the fiction of his son as an army officer, at the rank of captain, a splendid fellow, it was true, but almost unrecognisable. Now Neville was not sure what feelings he was pretending. Faced with these forthright orphans, with their whispering behind cupped hands and their adamantine stares, he realised that the speech he had long rehearsed had failed to impress. He twirled his elephant cane nervously. These children had a ruined, derelict aspect. He felt a little afraid of them. And they were supervised by a woman who looked as though life had stained her as a crude advertisement for misfortune.

Neville Brady had not settled in Australia as Honoria had. When he was a child the brilliant harbour seemed such an auspicious beckoning – he remembers himself filled up with a kind of adventurous jubilation; he remembers plunging into the dark sickroom where his sister lay, and dragging her up to the deck to see their New Beginning. The cliffs stretched to embrace the ship, the air was cool off the peaked water, workers were running along the dock, the long brown jetty grew and grew. Everything expanded. He clasped his sister's hand and squinted his eyes so that, in his swelling excitement, he would not overflow into tears. But within a year Neville's vision had begun to dessicate and contract; and in time he learned to resent his father's nation-changing decision. It left them all stranded, Neville thought. It made paternal meanness increase.

After an altercation George Brady withdrew his son from school, having decided, all things considered, it was a waste of time and money, and found him a position as an apprentice clerk at the harbourside firm of Woodruff and Blood, importers who supplied the colony with spices and cloth from the Indies, and familiar goods, chattels and foodstuffs from Home. Neville's work consisted chiefly in itemisation, counting stacked boxes and ticking off items, composing lists, cross-checking, adding long columns of large figures. It was dull beyond belief. The warehouses were ill-lit, bearing only high small windows, but also, in a strangely physical compensation, wonderfully scented. Neville would breathe in cloves, cinnamon, nutmeg, tea; he would press his face to jute sacks and dip his hands into wooden chests to rub an aroma into his palms and the tips of his fingers: Neville was a boy seeking to take into his body all the spice that was missing from his life.

In his boy's-own boredom he planned a straightforward

escape: he would purchase – with his own money – a passage to India. He would leave his father for ever. Honoria might be persuaded to join him, or he could send for her after he had made his fortune. Neville spent five long years at Woodruff and Blood. When he emerged, blinking like an animal that had been furled in hibernation, he was eighteen, furry and deranged by ambition, and his skin carried the faintly ineradicable scent of boxed-up spice. He took his stash of secret savings – all that he had not yielded to his father – and secured his passage. As he floated out of the harbour he could see his sister's pink dress – or did he imagine it? – in the shape of a lampshade, and felt so inexplicably bereft that he buried his head in the woolly dark privacy of his cape and, grown man that he was, wept boiling tears.

Lucy, Neville thought, looked very like his sister, but the boy Thomas could have been any mother's son, masquerading as a nephew. The girl's resemblance touched him – her triangular face, her curly dark hair – but she was also precociously wilful and fierce; she brandished a magnifying glass and had a pyromaniacal stare. For want of words, he coughed.

"Well, here we are then."

"Can I hold your elephant stick?" Lucy suddenly asked, bold as brass.

Thomas glared across at his traitorous sister.

"And would you like tea?" Mrs Minchin added.

Thomas switched his glare to the purple woman. He was concentrated and preoccupied, formulating Brazil. In his head long-limbed monkeys swung loops on jungle vines and screeched "Gold! Gold!" There were waterfalls, panthers and quick carnivorous fish. Bronze Indians, neat and featureless, looked on contentedly. Not this grubby fellow, this phoney uncle, who was so unlike their lost mother and so outrageously unkempt.

Over tea Neville presented Lucy with twelve violet glass bangles — six for each arm, he needlessly instructed — and to Thomas a small silver dagger, curved like the moon. Thomas instantly capitulated: *a silver dagger*. He had never been given so grown-up a gift, and was in a turmoil of mixed-up gratitude and distrust. Perhaps he would discuss Brazil with his uncle. Lucy had put aside the elephant stick and was sliding the twelve violet bangles up and down the length of her arms so that they chinked like twelve teaspoons against the sides of twelve teacups. From beneath her loose curly hair she smiled up at her brother. Thomas realised he had almost forgotten his sister's smile.

That night Thomas took the dagger with him to bed, and wondered half-awake what it must feel like to kill someone. Between the ribs, a deadly moon. ("Take that! Aargh!") He held it up in the darkness and saw it faintly. *Silver*. Bronze Indians, brassy sister, this silver weapon: all his imaginings were flaring metallic. He saw himself as a hero, keeping Lucy safe in a treacherous jungle. Ned. A gun. Sailing ships. Horseback. Charging fast-motioned at the unknown future. He felt he possessed a private world, which would one day soon materialise and invite him to enter. From the kitchen floated the sounds of Uncle Neville and Mrs Minchin in friendly conversation. Thomas listened as he grew sleepy, but they spoke their own over-syllabled, long-distance language: *Calcutta*, *Mahableshwar*, *Bombay*, *Hyderabad*. While he, already journeying, prepared to dream of Brazil.

Neville Brady was sleeping fitfully in his sister and brother-in-law's bed, and woke in the middle of the night to see his nephew standing in the centre of the room. The boy was naked and held before him the Indian dagger he had received as a gift. For an irrational second or two Neville thought that the boy had come to murder him — his earlier antipathy had been

68

so undisguised — but then he noticed his automatic movements and vacant eyes, the thin body tilted slightly in its state of suspension. Neville rose and led the boy gently, guiding him by the shoulders, back to his own bed, and felt in this act, however gratuitous, a first intuition of the existence of paternal tenderness. He uncurled the boy's fingers from the silver dagger, laid it on the floor, then lowered the child into the bed and pulled up the cover, smoothing and tucking it. Then, pausing again, he watched the boy sleep. The eyes were closed now, and the eyelids flickering. The face was pressed into the pillow at an awkward angle. The room was hushed — no wind outside, no-one astir — which made audible, just barely, the small boy's breathing.

"Honoria is dead," Neville Brady whispered to himself. "My sister, my lovely sister, Honoria, is dead."

How large the night was. A black shadow, sucking him in.

18

SHE WOULD LIE ON HER BACK IN THE WORLD OF SCURRYING ALIVE things — slaters, ants, earwigs, grasshoppers — and she would look up at the hard enamelled blue sky, and feel the sun on her cheeks, and see it as a pink-veined coin through her closed-up eyelids, and she would listen to leaves brush and rustle, and detect the light currents of a breeze — feeling the world as a princess feels a pea — and wonder why her adorable parents had died. Against the specificity of things leaned her own vague questionings; and against these small solidities, familiar and comfortable, a larger tenuousness. The world was untrustworthy. It held in cruel secret the possibility of erasure. *Death*, what an odd word, Lucy thought. *Death*, *breath*, she rhymed to herself. *Breath, death. Death, breath.* Her body carried trapped within it a sensation of shivering; even though the air was hot Lucy seemed to exist in a chilly grief-envelope. She tried hard to remember her mother's face, so that she might expel this unaccountable sensation, but already it was a vestige, already it was a hieroglyph. It could not be willed into vision. It could not be called, or fabricated. Instead she was met everywhere by involuntary and mostly trivial recursions. Once, having fed the chickens, her apron full of eggs, her boots plastered with grey muck, Lucy turned back to the house and caught sight of a pure white blouse, one of her favourites, flapping on the clothesline. It bounced as though it was electrically animated, the long sleeves waving. Lucy remembered her mother removing this blouse, pulling it up slowly over her head; but the garment snagged halfway, so her mother opened the buttons from the inside-out to reveal her face. Lucy had her arms held up, her girl-face peeped through its linen encasing, and she stayed like that, comically misshapen, for their mutual amusement. Just this small occasion. Just this scrap of a moment that in another time and other circumstances had no real employment as a memory. All this from the happenstance of a fluttering blouse, while she stood there with her lap of still-warm eggs, and her filthy boots, and her child's sad perplexion, all gathered together in a tiny tight loop of time.

What Lucy could remember were her mother's stories. They are now the matted fabric she clothes herself with, to try to smother her persistent shivers. Fairy stories. Childhood stories. Invented combinations. One of the stories is about a Dutchman and an Englishwoman. The Dutchman is a balloonist; he sails the world using the sky as his private ocean. Winds are his tides. Stars his companionable fishes. Night is the depthless wave that sweeps him smoothly along. When he sleeps, on turquoise silk cushions in the shape of fingers, and in a long wicker basket that looks like a Venetian boat, he looks upwards and spies a second black ocean. This man travels on his own unanchored dream which lists and uplifts, ripples and swoops, bucks, crests, glides luxuriantly along, all in the realm of an endlessly imponderable journey. (Lucy loved the way her mother would tell it, this crazy sailing. And she loved the embellishments: *turquoise silk cushions in the shape of fingers*.)

The Flying Dutchman is on a quest to seek a particular woman. She grew up in an ice cave and is known for the icy-pale translucence of her skin and for the ethereal quality of her character and intelligence. She bears a strawberry birthmark on the left side of her chest – just like Lucy – and is so sensitive to the world that she uncomfortably detects a single pea tucked away beneath mattresses. The woman is imprisoned in a small room in a palace in India; but has read of the anti-gravitational Dutchman, and planned her own rescue. She composes seductive messages, which she writes along the slippery lengths of satin ribbons, ties to pigeons and balloons, and then sends skyward, knowing they will find him. Floating endearments and invitations drift on the tidal winds. Longings-to-escape festoon the sky. So when the Dutchman, all alone, roams his oceanic space, accustomed to birds and clouds and the ornamentation of stars, he now meets sinuous sentences and multicoloured enticements. He steers his strange vessel in the direction of India, and systematically hovers over each one of its hundreds of palaces. One day the ice-woman looks up and there he is: it is magical; a sky-boat! It is her vision of liberation. She hastily writes a letter and ties it to a balloon, and up it goes, her freedom, her hope. The Dutchman is so excited to have at last found his journey's end – he has even glimpsed her pretty, shining face appearing at a starshaped window – that he leans forward a little carelessly to claim the letter, topples from his basket and plunges to the earth. The woman sees him falling, flailing and desperate, the unread letter clutched tightly in his hand. His body is crushed below her on tessellated paving stones, his bright blood channelled into diamonds and hexagons. The Venetian boat, captainless, sails slowly away. No-one knows where. And what became of the woman? Her window was bricked up as a punishment and in her isolation and darkness she eventually went insane. For a long time she held fast to the vision of the wicker boat in the sky, full of romance and possibility, full of various trans-portations, but by the end of her life saw only Mogul patterns of Dutch blood, glistening in the heat of Indian sunlight.

Lucy's mother changed the story many times, but the end, in every case, was never a happy one. The Dutchman missed his target, or found the wrong lover and was doomed to a miserable and mistaken partnership. Or a storm swept the basket to the top of Mount Ararat, and the Dutchman died there, stranded and lovelorn. Or he arrived too late, sliding on his belly through the star-window to discover the woman long dead from loss of hope. Or the Englishwoman grew old, continuously sending out messages; or she grew blind with her effort and wrote something indecipherable. In the worst version the ice-woman was so distressed by the tragedy of her unanswered ribbons that she set fire to her room, and burned down the palace around her, her face appearing one last time in a flaming star. The palace simply melted, Honoria said.

What shall Lucy do with her inheritance of story? Now she is left with a repertoire of exasperating desire, of hokum, memory, nonsense and tall-tale, that she has siphoned into herself as a stream of chill water. These stories fill her with an amorphous dissolving feeling. Even now, in the coin-light of warm summer sunshine, with her eyes closed and her mind bent on rational summoning, she is swept away and lost. And her mother's face is so vague it might be a wet footprint, shimmering thin as a breath, transient as a sundial shadow, poised on the very edge of complete disappearance.

19

LUCY WORE HER NEW WHITE BLOUSE AND HER NEW STRAW BONNET (topped with a posy of artificial violets), and carried on her arm her old herringbone coat; Thomas looked serious and grown-up in his best cap and stovepipe trousers and new navy serge jacket. Uncle Neville had arranged for the luggage to be sent ahead, so together they appeared as a group on a Sunday outing, all nervous expectation and dressed-up best-behaviour. The driver lifted Lucy by the waist to sit beside her brother, then Uncle Neville pulled himself up, setting the cart jolting and tilting with his awkward weight, and they perched there, all three, looking down at Mrs Minchin. To the children's horror she began to cry; they had never seen Mrs Minchin cry before. Her face smudged over and the tears gushed, and Ned, by her side, let out a long, plaintive howl. Up to this moment the children had been restless and flushed with excitement, but now they too collapsed and Uncle Neville, with no experience of wailing children and fulsome scenes of departure, looked alarmed in his *loco-parentis* incompetence. He was unused to these hyperbolic displays of emotion. Honoria, he recalled, had been a fantasist: she had clearly inspired in her children these crude and exorbitant performances.

In truth, Neville had been flattered by Arthur's request that he adopt the children. He had never met his brother-in-law, but since his life had been so far more or less dissolute, wrong-headed and fixedly geared to failure, he was pleased to be considered from a distance as parent material. Far from resenting the inflicted responsibility, Neville now saw his own role as heroic redemptor; the family tragedy required his intervention and confirmed his authority. In time, he believed, the two children would learn to respect him. He would be reformed, upright and a model substitute.

Neville retained a memory of Honoria he could not quite dispel: when he announced at eighteen that he was going to India, she laughed out loud. After all those years of sheer waiting and spiced-up visions, after all the adolescent torment of his own workaday isolation, he expected, at the very least, mute sisterly deference. But she threw her head back theatrically and laughed out loud and only later confessed that she was truly envious: "Have an adventure," she whispered, "have an adventure and I shall come flying over the ocean to join you."

Lucy and Thomas sat high on the cart and looked into the future. Their odd uncle beside them was silent and preoccupied. What they saw was all they had known sliding backwards into oblivion, and ahead, a gigantic, unknowable chaos. Lucy took Thomas's hand and it too was clammy. Sister and brother stared resolutely straight ahead. Without turning to look, they knew that behind them everything was already coated with the alluring patina of loss. It shone as it receded, like embers in a dying fire, and held for evermore the smouldering glint of their pasts.

20

The dock was bone coloured with weathering and stank of stale ocean. Wood had extraordinarily clear grain and looked more weighty than usual. The wind was salty, acute. The air held an amethyst tinge. Lucy gazed at the horizon and wondered why everyone's face seemed fluid and much less distinct than their harbourside surroundings. Perhaps travellers before a sea journey take on certain qualities of ocean, or at least respond in some way to the restless swell of parting tides. She could see mouths opening and closing and embraces exchanged. She could see Thomas and Neville in the distance, talking together to a sailor.

Lucy missed her parents. Lucy missed her dog. Around her neck hung the gold locket that contained her mother's face, rendered in black. If she were asked she would say: "Yes, I am an orphan, like a girl in a book, travelling with my brother and an uncle I barely know." She has devised this little speech so that it will guard and protect her, and make her seem more plausible and real in this wash of rowdy strangers. People were already heading up the gangplank and shouting back at the dock. Most were excited and loud and condescended to the crowd who would be left behind. Lucy wanted Thomas and Neville to return so that she could join this elect

76

group and head up to their place on the decks, up at the railing, looking down. She was worried that she might be pushed by the crowd into the harbour. She was worried that Thomas and Uncle Neville would not see her at all, and would decide conspiratorially to head off to England without her. Lucy could not remember ever being alone in a crowd before. It was both terrifying and exhilarating. She hid in her herringbone coat and imagined what it must be like never to be found. It must be like death. It must be like having a face that was a nothing, a mere cut-out in black, sealed where no-one in the world could see it.

When they were at last on the ship together, up high at the rusty, red-painted railing, Lucy and Thomas stood hand in hand — in biographical reversal and repetition — as Honoria and Neville had once done, approaching their New Beginning. Thomas pointed out that there were lovers shining mirrors at each other, one on the dock and one not far from them on the deck. It was the woman who was leaving. She tilted her oval mirror to catch at the sun and a young man, diminishing, answered from the shore. Lucy was transfixed. This was what she wanted, a photosensitive departure. Light trained by glass to locate and discover a face, a beam to travel on, a homing device, a sleek corridor through the infinity of sky itself.

PART TWO

"Knowledge comes only in flashes"

Walter Benjamin

21

THEY LEFT IN WINTER, SAILED FOR MONTHS, AND ARRIVED JUST IN TIME for a second winter. London uncannily opposed Melbourne on the spinning globe; it was half a planet away, the far side of things known, dark when the other was light, cold when the other was warm, yet consecutive seasons somehow registered its peculiar affinity. However, Lucy looked out from her high window onto the city that lay before her too vast, too chill and altogether too drear.

Stranger, she said to herself.

It was the scale of the place she could not assimilate: more roads and laneways than any girl could remember, thousands of chimneys jutting at the sky, buildings, endless buildings, with complicated façades like frowning faces with sightless eyes. The air was a brown and choking vapour: Londoners walked with their faces angled towards the ground, as if smoke and fog had a weight that pressed down upon their heads. All was weltering gloom. All looked infernal, oppressive. December rain fell quietly in failing light and Lucy's spirits, damp and wintry, also tumbled and fell.

Their dwelling was a modest house of two levels in Camden Town. The children each attended a local school, and were each bullied and teased, almost unceasingly, because of their accents. Thomas returned from his first day at school with a bloody nose and Lucy's long hair had been dipped into Indian ink: they both bore on their clothes spotted patterns that announced their contemptible foreignness. Lucy had believed that orphans were the object of pity, but at school she was again and again disproven; she battled daily with insult and casual denunciation. Thomas and Lucy invented a series of truancies. Their games were for each other, their child community, just two.

Uncle Neville had taken the children on tours around the centre, but somehow this confirmed its unreality. The Houses of Parliament, London Bridge, the Tower of London: each was too monumental to be anything other than fictitious. They loomed sombre, full of great and terrible histories, they squatted by the Thames with intimidating command, their upper reaches swallowed by obliterating sky. Thomas told Lucy that the Tower contained buckets-of-blood; he scared her with his idiosyncratic re-tellings of British history and his rediscovered pleasure in tales of the macabre. Thomas beheaded so many old queens and princesses that Lucy felt herself quake for all the violence that bodies might attract. One day – on their way to visit Neville in the company office – they paused together on windy Blackfriars Bridge and Lucy by accident discovered a way to contest him. Somewhere down below, beyond the turbulent water, a woman on the riverbank began suddenly to sing; she lifted her voice and began an aria. Her song rose upwards in a string of beaded notes and resonated in the deep shadowy space formed by the stone walls of the embankment. When Lucy bent over to look she could see a hatless blonde woman in a frilly costume, holding her arms outstretched and performing to the river. The words may have been Italian; in any case Lucy heard something from within the body that was sweet, pure and given as a gift. Something which repudiated physical hurt. Something for which there was no equivalence and no particular image.

"Lunatic," said Thomas, with a little smirk.

He tugged at Lucy's hand.

But Lucy was entranced. She raised her gaze and saw then the black sooty dome of St Paul's, fat as a breast and incontrovertible, and wondered whether there might be things that only girls and women know.

When they rode home atop the afternoon coach with Neville, Lucy considered saying something, to try to formulate whatever was resting, cloudy and inchoate, on the very fringe of her consciousness, but could not find the words. From their perch she could watch the massive head of the black horse, snorting and jerking and bobbing in front, and the driver with his high hat, scratching with dirty fingernails at the back of his neck. Neville was fidgeting with papers, trying to put them in order, and Thomas was employed picking the satin label from the inside of his Irish cap. Lucy knew herself double: these details – the horse, the cap, the dirty fingernails – were plaited stubbornly with the most imprecise intuitions. These details, the *so particular* nature of things, seemed to lodge in some ephemeral equation she could not calculate or figure. The commandment of ordinary things to look, and the countervailing sense of the world's detachment, troubled and distressed her. Lucy wondered how she might tell this, or to whom.

That first dreadful winter Lucy's nose became red and her hands were permanently frozen. Thomas turned blue and watery, and even Neville, staunchly Anglophile, expressed anguished longings for tropical India and the humane primrose tint of a non-English sun. Both children developed rattly chests and throaty voices as cold air settled like mist in their Antipodean bodies, and Neville was obliged to learn improved forms of tenderness as a nurse. He waited at their bedsides with handkerchiefs and balm, told funny stories about his childhood, and read aloud from Dickens as the invalids settled for bedtime. The brand-new serial, *Great Expectations*, unfolded each night – "his best yet!" – a story driven by the tremulous anxiety of destiny unknown. Thomas called himself Pip for a while, but Lucy too wanted to be Pip and resented his claim. The novel made London seem altogether more actual and they were all delighted that Dickens had mentioned Australia: it validated an existence others here took as vague conjecture. When Lucy looked at Australia on the map, it was a fat anomalous island, loosely adrift by itself, with that bit sticking up on the right that had no reason to be there and looking like someone at school with their hand up, but with the wrong answer to the question. Nevertheless the shape pleased her, so she looked at it again, cross-eyed, and it pleased her still.

"Do you think", she asked Thomas, "that we have Great Expectations?"

"Of course," he replied. "Don't forget Brazil."

And Lucy tried hard to not forget what she had never remembered.

There was a moment – it was all so simple – that Lucy and Thomas simultaneously realised that they loved Uncle Neville, and that they had somehow all managed to make a life in London together.

Outside their bedroom window night-life was busy in the street. Carts, vendors, the lively commerce of rich and poor. A raucous voice beneath their window shouted "Ott chestnuts! Chestnuts ott!" and a sweet roasting fragrance immediately followed the sound. Then, as if on cue, Neville appeared at the doorway with a brown paper bag of roasted chestnuts. He held it aloft, like a trophy, and grinned towards them.

"Ott chestnuts!" he called out.

He shook water from his shoulders, like a dog, then filled the room with his body.

Neville sat on the edge of the bed and shared the chestnuts precisely, counting one-two-three, one-two-three, as children do. For the first time Lucy and Thomas saw Neville's resemblance to their mother — something in the angle of the lamplight and his oblique posture on the bed — and they looked at each other reassured and with instinctive understanding.

"What larks!" Neville exclaimed. Then, mimicking further: ". . . 'there certainly were a peck of orange peel. Partickler when he see the ghost'!"

This was their private three-way joke.

In *Great Expectations* Joe Gargery, the country father-figure, honest and uneducated, has been to his first theatrical performance — of *Hamlet*. Pip asks, "Was there a great sensation?" and Joe answers charmingly, according to his senses: the odour of orange peel. The children had needed the joke explained, and Neville thereafter enjoyed replaying the phrase.

"Partickler!" Lucy repeated as Neville said goodnight. He doffed an invisible cap, having discovered in himself, through the agency of the children, hidden resources of play as well as parenthood.

"Partickler!" he echoed. "'Partickler when he see the ghost'!"

When she is an adult and loves London Lucy will discover a drawing of St Paul's Cathedral she sketched in her first miserable year in the city. The drawing is unbalanced and inept, an insecure shape, but still recognisable and lovingly executed. St Paul's does not appear, after all, like a giant breast. It appears like a bulbous lamp, pendant from the sky. And although it is dark and begrimed, it carries within it, Lucy thinks, a suppressed ivory glow. It is the light of that one, that very first, that *partickler* London winter, the winter which held the promise of three lives thawing into newness.

22

LOOKING BACK ON THOSE YEARS IN LONDON, SEVEN IN ALL, SHE THINKS of it not so much as a novelistic concatenation of events, the way people conventionally describe movement from childhood to adulthood, logical, sequential, cementing identity more firmly, but as an irregular sequence of *Special Things Seen*. Lucy kept a private diary, bound in purple morocco and tied with a black ribbon, in which she recorded and stored her apprehensions not of events, but of images. Unable to reason her profound sense of discrepancy in the world, discrepancy between bodies and words, between the niggardly specificity of things, often tiny, inconsequential, mundane things – a reflection in a puddle, laurel trees wildly waving, Thomas's face emerging scrubbed and reddened from an unwrapping towel – and the cloudy abstractions they brought in their wake, she decided she would know the world by its imagistic revelations. Seen this way, London presented a venerable randomness, by which, eventually, Lucy was won over.

Dead Prince Albert:

In 1861, the year of her arrival in London, Prince Albert, Victoria's consort, died in the middle of the winter in which Lucy's chest first began to fail. Queen Victoria was already in public mourning for her mother, the Duchess of Kent, who had died earlier that year, in March. Neville read from *The Times*: the Prince Consort, he announced, "has been suddenly snatched from us". The children were alarmed by the euphemistical "snatched", which seemed nasty, infantile and stupidly cruel. What does it mean to be "snatched"? When she came to write in her diary Lucy recorded the newspaper image of Albert's face in a black-bordered rectangle, boxed in a portrait-coffin, sealed up in the solemn space of the irretrievably snatched. He looked dull and his eyes were filmy and unfocused, as though he peered through the veil of Victoria's tears.

Were her parents snatched?

The blind woman:

She stood on a corner, almost every day, not very far from where they lived. Her eyeballs were milky white, and around her neck hung a sign saying BLIND — in case one couldn't guess — and a small medallion which officially licensed her to beg. She had a tired lined face, but seemed unaccountably cheerful. When Lucy recorded the blind woman she thought of the oval face above a triangular shawl, and the medallion glinting with more spark than the round white eyes. That this woman resolved to shapes was Lucy's protection: she could not bring herself to imagine the darkness there, the loss of every composition that the living eye could construct.

One day Lucy saw the blind woman being led by a girl her age. The woman had her hand on the girl's head and was being guided through her darkness. Perhaps the girl was her daughter. Perhaps, like Mrs O'Connor, there were seeing dreams and brave assertions in this difficult city.

The magic-lantern show:

There were so many of these, so many slide shows in dim halls fuelled by limelight or gas. In the darkness impossible images rose flourishing before them: the pyramids of Egypt, the temples of India, stories of war and revolution, scenes of horror and beauty. Lucy recorded the Niagara Falls, tinted pea green and azure, gushing towards them in a stream of heavy light; she recorded Turkish dancers with sinuous bellies (the men behind her hooted and cheered); she recorded a Chinaman in a peaked hat, carrying two buckets on a stick. This last image she cherished because it connected in some way with her father, but she did not dwell on the significance of something so imprecise. Instead she rejoiced in the arbitrariness of all she had seen, thinking it a thrill to envision so much, and so unexpected.

The door handle:

A reflection of her own face, curved on a brass doorhandle. It was edged by a kind of scroll and wonderfully distorted. Lucy moved her face so that it slid around the knob of the handle and saw herself — a shy girl of fourteen now, self-conscious, misplaced, entranced by mirrors — remade, almost convincingly, as a fluent golden spirit.

The stereoscope:

Uncle Neville took the children to Covent Garden to see T.W. Williams' Stereoscope Exhibition. They peered into movable viewing binoculars at a doubled photograph, which by some trick of vision transformed to three dimensions. A stuffed cockatoo, arranged with still life (an oriental vase, curtains, tassels, a carved ball), was a frozen marvel: objects rotund, detailed and dense enough to touch sprang forward from the flat and otherwise unremarkable image. Lucy saw in this simple technological effect both the photograph and its disremembering, implicit morbidity and a fake life-likeness.

Three hyacinths:

Just that. Three sapphire-blue hyacinths in a single clay pot. They had the gravity of monuments and the perfection of Eden. And they had veins like strings, like those in old human hands.

The baby's head:

She had seen a beggar on the street, a girl not much older than herself, sitting on the footpath with a baby on her lap. The beggar held the baby in some particular way, at some very intimate and loving angle, that revealed its head as a fraction, as a sickle moon rising. Lucy reached into her pockets and gave the mother her single halfpenny, but would have given much more, in gratitude for whatever stirring intuition or clairvoyance or memory had moved her.

The bristle workers:

At the end of their street was a bristle factory: it manufactured scrubbing brushes and brooms in vast prickly quantities. Lucy saw women workers arriving early in the morning in friendly twos and threes, chattering as they entered the wide wooden doors of the building. In the evening she saw them again, sweeping out in larger groups, appearing subdued and exhausted. What she noticed was their hands. Some wore bandages of white linen, and held their hands up, a little way from their bodies, carrying bags and parcels on their hefty arms. Under the lamplight the large hand-shapes looked almost inhuman. Lucy had no idea what toil the women performed, but saw simply this, that they left the factory, with soft golden light spilling out behind them, looking damaged and worn. It was a small community of women with painful hands.

The glass sheep:

They went to church very rarely, and then to the modest one around the corner with its white-framed brickwork, its weekly homily pasted, pathetically proclaiming, on a board at the front, and its bent metal spire, which held up a sad cross with vandalised spokes. They went for some reason Lucy has long since forgotten and sat bored, resentful and inattentive. Even Neville could hardly pretend his devotion. But a sudden shaft of light from outside hit a window of Christ and his flock, and the sun was instantly visible in the belly of a kneeling sheep. The stained Christ was lovely, as were the wheat sheaves and the clouds and the spikes of green grass, but only the humble sheep appeared truly supernatural, conveying the entire sun in its semi-transparent body. Lucy turned her rapt face towards it and thought to herself: this is God's language; he speaks in gatherings of light.

23

IN THEIR FIRST FIVE YEARS OR SO IN LONDON THEY SURVIVED
tolerably well. Neville worked at the company, Woodruff and
Blood; Thomas and Lucy went intermittently to school; and
they all managed their new lives by mutual strategies of hard
work, and the suppression of mourning. But in 1866, when
Lucy was fourteen, Neville was shamefully dismissed from his
position as a clerk; he had been embezzling funds and gambling
them, with regular unsuccess, on various loopy schemes and
dodgy propositions. It was only his long service to the company
that saved him from debtors' prison; besides, he was known
as a jolly-good-fellow and an altogether-charming-chap, and
thus only, it seemed, incidentally crooked. The family moved
to smaller rooms in the cramped East End, and everything
they had known once again shifted: Thomas and Lucy must
both seek work; and Neville — who claimed in sorrowful tones
that all he knew about was spices — was obliged to take whatever odd jobs came his way.

Something in Neville Brady crazed and cracked open. He felt
alien in the world, and dislocated. He concocted schemes and
designs — to open his own spice-importation business, to immi-
grate to Canada under a false name, to return to Australia. He
would be like Magwitch, he thought, inventing his own Great

Expectations, falling out of visible history into secret possibilities. But unfunded, Neville's concoctions remained distant hopes. Instead, with time on his hands and a sense of inner collapse, he turned to spiritualism of various forms to assure and reconnect him to whatever spirited self he had once, long ago, inhabited: the child who ran along the ship deck, whooping with joy in the sunshine, expecting New Beginnings. Neville attended public talks on phrenology, mesmerism and Eastern religions, on palmistry, seances and gaseous experimentation. He sent away for pamphlets on do-it-yourself divination, scrying and life-after-death experiences. All manner of ghost-trapping and necromancy obsessed him. More specifically, Neville conceived the idea that he must communicate with Honoria: that her untimely death and lost infant and the dreadful consequences with Arthur, meant that something in the order of things, the immemorial order, was out of kilter, out of joint, and dangerously unquiet.

One morning Neville told the children of a medium, Madame d'Esperance, whose special talent was for summoning the tragically dead. "Ectoplasm!" declared Neville; "it is ectoplasm ghosts are composed of." The children eyed their uncle suspiciously as he described an account on a handbill of spirit-world happenings: dead parents and grandparents, uncles and aunts, even next-door neighbours and favourite pets, had been conjured out of thin air at Madame d'Esperance's seances.

"The *gift*," said Neville, with a fanatical tone. "She has the gift of seeing. Do you understand?"

Lucy and Thomas did not understand. They were embarrassed more by Neville's new enthusiasm than by his loss of work.

It was a thin still evening, flimsy as gauze, when Lucy accompanied Neville, holding his quivering hand, to Madame d'Esperance's Salon of Spiritual Experience. There were three other customers, all nervy and earnest looking, and a maid servant bade them seat themselves at a round covered table. Candles were extinguished, then Madame made her entrance with a single candle held beneath her chin, so that she looked as if she wore a mask and was already lodged at some halfway point between the animate and the inanimate worlds. She appeared, thought Lucy, as if she would have a better claim with worlds infernal, than heavenly; Lucy suspected this bogus profundity and dramatic mien. In an accent of no known nation Madame commanded the participants link their little fingers in a circle around the table and then with great ceremony blew out the remaining candle.

At this point Lucy became intrigued and excited. In the darkness the others appeared as dapples in a penumbral gloom, shades of people rather than individuals, already transported in their simple and credulous sincerity to the outlandish realm in which linked bodies and gutted candles opened doors almost instantly to the space of death. Someone coughed and someone else bumped the table with an elbow. Anxieties, fantasies, wrenched and deformed griefs, hung as miasma in the air between them.

Before the session Madame d'Esperance had asked her clients to whom they wished to speak, and had elicited slim details and scraps of personal information. One man, a Mr Talbot, a fat weepy widower, was the first communicant, and when the medium summoned his wife she came as a high squeaking voice, issuing with shrill insistence from a corner of the room.

"Tubby!" she called. "Tubby, my love!" (for that was what Talbot had said she used to call him), adding, "for my sake marry again, within the year."

It was a clear instruction. Lucy heard a gasp of recognition, and imagined Tubby relieved, even delighted, at his ghost-wife's sound and compassionate advice. The other couple, the elderly Gillams, seeking their lost daughter, were told in straight-forward and no uncertain terms that Miriam was invisibly present, floating somewhere nearby, but could only be contacted directly if they returned tomorrow evening. Lucy heard Mr Gillam hush his wife and saw their shapes lean together in commiseration.

When it was their turn Lucy could feel Neville stiffen beside her. Madame d'Esperance slumped in her chair then rose up again, and called out "Honoria, Honoria," stretching the vowels to excruciating length. And then, to their horror, an apparition appeared.

"Ectoplasm," whispered Neville.

There was a wavery light, like a reflection from water, and an imprecise face appeared slowly within it, the blurry outlines of eyes and a small mouth, a shadowy nimbus of hair, and a face-shape, definitely a face-shape, drifting high above them, somewhere near the ceiling. It did not speak or communicate, but hovered there in an implicitly posthumous flare, claim-ing to be the revenant Honoria Strange.

"Behold me!" it commanded.

Although Lucy knew in her heart of hearts that this was not her mother, and imagined devious trickery and hidden contraptions, she was nevertheless captivated by the summon-ing of such a luminous image. It hung for half a minute or so, an entirely peculiar vision, screened by some inscrutable means unknown, to produce this single liquid face. Lucy heard Uncle Neville let out a sob. Then another, then another, until he had broken the magic circle and dropped his head onto the table. The face disappeared and Madame d'Esperance lit the candle, then pronounced the seance successful and at an end. She said Neville must come again if he wished to hear his dead sister speak.

"Tomorrow," she repeated. He must come again tomorrow.

When Lucy told Thomas about the seance later that night, they agreed it was specious, fraudulent and probably downright criminal.

"'Partickler when he see the ghost'!" Thomas joked.

But then he felt almost immediately ashamed of himself; mocking Neville was too disloyal. Besides, he had seriously wondered about whether his parents might exist as ghosts, and remembered seeing his father's face, violence-distressed and godforsaken, resting after his death on the hallway mirror. Thomas was too afraid to test his secret speculations. He wished he had not seen the face on the mirror. And he wished he had not told Lucy what he had seen. It was something that would follow him all his life, like having the wrong person's shadow, like carrying an aberration of presence, like dragging into the bright living world some heavy taint of the grave.

On Lucy's second and last visit with Neville to the Salon, Madame d'Esperance employed a planchette. Lucy had never heard of these instruments before: it was a thin piece of wood, shaped in a stretched triangle and mounted on small wheel castors with a pencil affixed to one end, pointing downwards. This device automatically wrote messages from somewhere beyond: it slid around the table, with Madame's guiding hand, forming letters in spidery spirit handwriting. When Madame d'Esperance revealed the message it was completely illegible. There was possibly a T, and possibly a Y, and a word that might, Mr Gillam thought, have spelled out "mustard". Madame d'Esperance offered various inventive interpretations, but suggested Neville should return to use the little viewing eye of the planchette, which could be swept over a printed sheet of letters. In this way, she claimed, spirit messages — unimpeded — were spelled more precisely.

* * *

Lucy dreamed that her mother left scrawled and unreadable messages in dust on the surface of a hallway mirror. Her mystic writing pad. And for many years, on and off, she thought about the seance, and the make-believe face, and the unreliable planchette. She could not forget the anonymous image stretched like a sail upon the ceiling, or Uncle Neville's impassioned sobbing, given up for what he truly believed was his younger sister, recomposed above them, bright and imperative.

24

THOMAS, NOW SIXTEEN, WAS APPRENTICED TO A COOPER, A JOB HE found tiresome and almost demeaning. Unlike his employer, he could read and write, and thought it absurd that Uncle Neville had arranged things thus, so that he bent wood all day in heat-moulded curves, and held copper rings at the blazing forge, and shovelled away shit from beneath the carthorses. But Neville assured him that it was a short-term measure, a stopgap, he said, until he received sure intelligence of the future from Honoria, from the wise, all-knowing zone in which she now had her being. Neville saw the world simply bisected, the living and the dead, still communing, still corresponding, still offering each other advice, but despite his expensive visits to Madame d'Esperance's Salon, he had yet to discover how to rescue the children from the predicament into which he had cast them.

After only a month at the cooper's, Thomas learned the necessity of initiative and found his own employment, together with an advance in salary to break his indenture. He presented himself at Mr Martin Childe's Magic Lantern Establishment, and pronounced himself desirous of a career in the projection of images. Mr Martin Childe was a barrel-shaped man — he might, indeed, have been fashioned by a cooper — who wore corduroy trousers and jacket and a neck scarf tied like a flower. He quizzed Thomas on the reason for his attraction to lantern technology and found in the boy a kindred spirit: both loved, above all, the phantasmagoria, the gruesome narratives of horror, spooks and unseemly violence, and neither, it seemed, enjoyed the Temperance slide shows, or the long, pious sequences on The Life of Christ in Palestine. Mr Childe thought Thomas respectable, intelligent and of excellent taste: he offered him a repast of corned beef and sherry and then employment at various tasks – taking admission, sweeping the auditorium, learning, by stages, the mechanisms of gas jets and lenses and star-dissolving taps (whatever they were). He held rectangles of images up to the window and demonstrated the rudimentary physics and optics by which lantern slides, hand-painted on glass, were enlivened by airy expansion into public vision. They shook hands vigorously as Thomas departed.

"Master Strange," said Mr Childe – who relished Thomas's surname and used it frequently – "welcome, my boy, to the Childish Establishment!" Thomas could hardly believe his luck. He ran home along the High Street, whooping and leaping like a boy on a deck, and burst into their small rooms to greet Lucy and Neville with his eyes fired up and aglow, lively and bedazzling, like twin gas flames at an eight o'clock magic-lantern show.

25

LUCY COULD NOT BRING HERSELF TO SEEK WORK IN THE BRISTLE factory, although the turnover was high and they often had positions vacant. She was disturbed by the thought of damage to her hands, even though she longed — in a way she could not even identify — for a small community of sympathetic women. She was not well educated enough to apply for work as a governess, and had virtually no skills that would recommend her to an employer. The idea of working as a nanny did not appeal, nor did she wish to be a domestic servant.

Lucy found work at last in an albumen factory. Albumen, she discovered, was the substance used in the manufacture of photographic paper, and it was obtained, quite simply, from the white of eggs. When she first applied for the position, she met a woman with a huge bosom — a Mrs McTierney — who tested her ability to crack open eggs. Lucy was given six eggs and instructed to part them cleanly, as if she were performing an operation on a living being. She was fastidious and quick: she passed the test. Mrs McTierney said that usually girls were nervous when she watched, and often wrecked or spilled at least one or two. She fingered the ruffles of her blouse and looked at Lucy sternly.

"I'm never nervous," Lucy heard herself declare. "It's not in my nature."

It was true. She suddenly knew it. She was never nervous.

At work Lucy sat at a long bench with twenty-three other women (two-dozen-hard-eggs, they joked), each with a mountain of stacked eggs at their side and a kind of trough between them. Together the women spent the day separating yolks and whites, whites and yolks, so that the viscous shiny liquid filled a pool before them. They had vigilantly to check for blood or yolk in the white, and to watch, necessarily, for shell and rottenness. Egg odour entered their skin and hair, and sticky matter stained their work aprons and pinafores; but otherwise the job was easy and even meditative. Sometimes the women worked silently, cracking eggs side by side, each enclosed in her own sealed and uncracked thoughts; more often, however, they chattered together. Once a week each contributed a farthing to hire a reader, who sat alongside them, reading aloud from serials, or newspapers, or collections of short stories. Words circulated in the air like a new kind of energy, in waves and particles, focused and diffuse, showing and obscuring what might exist in the world. Lucy loved the timbre of the reader's voice and her habit of clicking her teeth with her tongue at her own points of concern in the narrative.

Mrs McTierney supervised, strolling slowly, her hen-like bosom swelling before her.

The workers were now-and-then rotated to different tasks, so that Lucy had also the job of whisking the albumen in drums to a high bubbly froth, or tipping the liquid into storage for fermentation. Most of all she liked to work with the paper. A single sheet was dipped and floated in albumen solution, then hung up to dry. Lastly it was rolled and sorted into piles of first- or second-grade paper. Everything about this process of labour stank, but it had about it the pre-industrial gratification of completion, of an entire act of manufacture, seen through to the packages neatly addressed and sent away to photographers.

Years later Lucy found herself using the albumen paper that she and her co-workers may have produced. It was a moment of such profound memory retrieval that with it came the sour smell of fermented albumen and recalled to her the faces of all the women she had loved. She held the paper to the light to discover its grade and to inspect it for streaks or tiny cracks; she rubbed it between her fingertips and assessed the quality of the surface and gloss, checking to see if it was single or double-dipped, and knew at that moment that honourable work returns itself in these stray unguessable circuits; some random experience of labour returns as good tidings; some object sent into the world, blank, potential, arrives as the fortunate component of wholly new meanings.

Years later, too, Lucy flicked through her diary of *Special Things Seen*, and saw that on her first day at work in the albumen factory she had left at four o'clock in the afternoon, and recorded that the sky was the colour of a sheet of photographic paper, drenched in wet egg-white, a bright screen, gleaming lightly as it hung to dry.

26

"STRANGE," SHE SAID TO THOMAS, "HOW FICTION PREDICTS."

In *Great Expectations* there is an episode in which Pip, having newly come into his fortune, goes to a tailor to have a fine suit fitted. A boy there, Trabb's boy, treats him with insolence, sweeping the floor by banging the broom at every corner, scowling, getting in the way, physically dissenting from and mocking the hero's changed circumstances. Lucy thought of this episode when she began work at the albumen factory, except that her own situation was a kind of reversal. The women at the factory knew that she could read and write and were alerted every time she opened her mouth — with that peculiar cross-planetary accent of hers — that she was not one of them and was lodged for some reason in the wrong class and work. At first they knocked or slapped her with relaxed and easy malice as they passed, and one deliberately flicked an egg from the top of her pile, so that it smashed across her shoes and she was obliged to apologise to Mrs McTierney and waste time cleaning up. They joked about her name: "she's a strange one," they said, and excluded her from their friendly conversation.

All this altered when one day a fierce man came to the factory. He was large and ill-kempt, with a shock of orange hair. He stood at the doorway demanding to see one of the workers,

Rose; he hollered her name and emanated a threatening presence. Rose was a small woman, no more than five feet tall, who was cowered and abused by her much larger husband. Mrs McTierney was at the back of the room and stood her ground, asking the man immediately to leave, but Lucy, acting on impulse, moved forward at once to meet and confront him. She saw his face strewn with whiskers and his irrational glare.

"This is ungentlemanly, sir," she boldly declared — speaking in a voice that sounded stage-hall and melodramatic — "you must leave. Now."

The man was dumbfounded for a second: he simply stared. He had wild black eyes and alcoholic breath. Then he swung his arm in a wide arc and using tremendous force struck Lucy across the face with the back of his hand. She fell heavily, taking with her a nearby stack of eggs and detonating at least twenty in a messy explosion. The floor was blazoned with yellow and white commingled, and Lucy lay on her side, stunned and stinging, with the sharp taste of blood flooding into her mouth. Pain overtook her stagey illusion.

The man then turned on his heel and left, and Rose, standing half-hidden, fell away into a faint.

After that the women's behaviour carried an air of propitiation. They were considerate, kind and included Lucy in their talk. They forgave her accent and gathered her into a quiet receptive embrace in which she experienced deliberate tenderness and everyday solidarity. From these women Lucy at last learned about female knowledge: she learned about miscarriages, recipes, home remedies and local gossip; she learned about the delectable and frightening otherness of men, about the arbitrariness of love and the glorious delirium of passion. All this from her foolish bravery and her face battered, leaking blood, lying sideways in a thin pool of broken eggs, which resembled so many smashed-up and still-glistening lights.

Three months later, Rose was murdered by her violent husband. The details were not at all theatrical. He broke her head with an ale bottle, confident in his brutal, annihilating authority. The women asked Lucy — "bein' that she was educated an' all" — to give a little speech about Rose's passing. It was a ritual of the workplace. A system of formal mourning. Lucy stood at the head of the troughs of collected white and spoke of the pain of being hit and the fellowship of women. She told them of her parents' deaths, and how something holy attaches to grief. She said there is a glow to love: she had actually seen it. It is like the entire sun coming to rest in the belly of a kneeling sheep. It is like a glint from the beads of an Italian necklace that hung at her mother's throat. It is like two lovers flashing mirrors through space and time. Some of the women wept. There was a chorus of muffled sobbing behind Lucy's words and throughout the hall a warm atmosphere of shared distress. Lucy said, last of all, that this glow defeats the fist that swings cruelly to strike a face and the poison that creeps up into mothers' wombs. It is a miraculous light, a light that carries the amazement of seeing a falling star plunge at night into the ocean. Lucy fell silent. She was not sure she believed it. She was a fourteen-year-old girl describing life, in an egg-filled factory hall to a group of weeping women. But the blessedness of the moment — even then she knew it — was in its simple saying, in finding the right words.

Lucy worked at the albumen factory for almost two years. This was a place she sheltered in. When she left she still retained her Australian accent and was still, after all, distinctively *strange*. She could not make a speech. The women embraced her, one by one, in a sorrowful ceremony, and Mrs McTierney handed her a single brown egg, as a parting gift. It was warm and lovely, equal to their silence.

27

CLIMBING, AS IN A DREAM. CLIMBING THE STEEP STAIRS WITH A SINGLE candle quivering under the breath of night. There he is, her brother Thomas, sleepwalking again. She brings the light to his face and sees that he is otherworldly and implacably absent. She knows he communes with ghosts. She knows he meets in this nomadic state, this shadowy night wandering, the father and mother she herself never manages to see. She knows she is cheated, as Neville too, in his own private anguish, consulting mendacious voices and tricksy visions, is also cheated.

28

NEVILLE HANDED LUCY A SMALL DAGUERREOTYPE. IT WAS IN A BRASS
and velvet case and unlocked with a miniature key. The image
inside was of a good-looking young man; he faced the camera
at an angle and had an honest stare, a firm jaw and an
impressive black moustache.

"Isaac Newton," Neville said. "Named, of course, for the
physicist."

Lucy looked again at Isaac Newton, dark-faced and phos-
phorescent in his glassed-in square. He was unexceptional. The
portrait and its devices reduced him to a merely generic
gentleman, fixed in a doleful closet of perpetual night. She
closed the case and locked him up.

In India Neville had worked with Isaac Newton. He was a
decent fellow, said Neville, clean-living and seeking matri-
mony, and had solicited his old friend's aid in securing a wife.

Neville paused and waited for Lucy to respond.

"I thought", he went on, "that you might consider an
alliance with my friend, Isaac Newton."

Neville could not disguise an almost pleading tone.

"I owe him money," he added. "You only have to meet him,
Lucy, and then you could return. No obligation. No obligation
at all."

"Return?"

"Return from India. Back to London."

Lucy faced her uncle. "You want me to go to India?"

Neville was looking old. The hair at his forehead was grey and his face was ageing, as some do, into states of fixed frown and confirmed perplexion. He shaved less frequently and was ashamed to be supported in middle-age, in such reduced circumstances, by his young niece and nephew. His neckties had begun to show evidence of carelessly dropped food. Unemployment left him smeary, unmade and dishevelled.

"No obligation," he meekly repeated. "Madame d'Esperance has consulted your mother . . ."

So it is, by these small interceptions loaded with possibility, by others' agency or possibly ignoble intentions, that destinations present themselves and lives shift direction. Sometimes this is what we are unknowingly awaiting: to be taken up by the motion of some charismatic moment, some accidental, odd, or contingent opportunity. It is like love, or desire – the swerving acceleration, the fast-motioning skid. We wait, all of us, for what enlivens and unsettles us. It took Lucy only half an hour to make up her mind: she would travel alone to India to meet this boxed version of Isaac Newton, this man who shone with unearthly light from his sealed brass compartment. *Alone*, thought Lucy. It was an immense idea. Thomas had no wish to chaperone his sister: he was settled at Childe's and bent on newfangled experimentation; and Neville was too demoralised, he said, for journeys or excursions.

Plans, shopping, the acceleration of time.

The month before Lucy left London everything existed magnified and in a state of intensification. The promise of travel releases essences and glazes everything with Expectations. Women at the factory confided things they might not otherwise have told her, and were enjoined by the excitement of going-to-India. One of them asked her to send an embroidered shawl. Another brought along a map that had belonged to her father: it showed India encrusted with names, mountains, sinuous rivers. India was shaped like a ghost-writing planchette, pointing mysteriously at the green-painted ocean.

As Lucy's departure grew nearer, Thomas became anxious. He may have felt guilty about his enthralment to the Childish Establishment; in any case he began to fret about Lucy's venture. One day he came home with a cholera belt, a portable medicine kit and an ugly hard hat framed by an insect net, and later added pamphlets on travellers' advice for the East and a phial of yellow liquid a merchant claimed – one hundred per cent! – cured all tropical fevers. Then Thomas developed rough coughing in spasms, as his father had once developed a crimson-coloured skin. What could not be uttered was played out in these practical gifts, and in the sense of physical vulnerability when he imagined his sister gone.

Lucy departed in early morning under a threatening sky. She waved from the high deck, astonished at her own embarking – all by herself, *alone* – for Bombay, India. A small group of women from the factory flapped their handkerchiefs. Neville was teary and dabbed his eyes with a stripy scarf, and Thomas was seized by a fit of sudden coughing. Lucy watched them fuss together in an instinct of mutual comfort. She saw them recede, gradually blurring into docklands and the left-behind crowd, and then, just before they became at last indistinguishable, she saw Neville's hat blow off, an upswept dot, and Thomas run to the very dock-edge to lean over and retrieve it. At that point she wept. Lucy wept because they had, after all, made a life together: three stranded colonials wedded in a makeshift family, represented now in this triangle, growing distended and more acute, as she floated away into a story that would be hers alone.

29

IT IS SOMETHING PECULIAR, LUCY DECIDED, ABOUT OCEAN TRAVEL, that one feels one has always done it. On a ship it is impossible to believe you ever had a life on land; the pitch of the deep sea, the state of being buoyed, these begin to feel like the unalterable and persistent state of being. She loved the murmurous waves and the sensation of perpetual motion. She enjoyed the tilted horizon, the smell of wet canvas and rope, the sound of sailors' quick feet slapping at the deck, the occasional slip of a glass across an angled table, the rocking of hammocks and curtains in gravitational adjustment: the whole disquiet of ships was an unending marvel. Most of all, however, Lucy loved the night, and when they were in the middle of the ocean they might have been sailing in sky. The stars were multiplied and everywhere extensive, and sparks on the ocean appeared as sunken reflections. In her private notebook of *Special Things Seen*, Lucy devoted almost ten pages to the oceanic night sky. It was like a glimpse of creation expanded; it filled her with awe and an impulse to artistry. She wanted to memorise it all, to reprint water and sky as her own wavy marks on paper.

Every night, as a kind of ritual, Lucy went to the deck after most of the passengers had retired, and watched the dark. She became familiar with constellations and tracked their slow swipe across the heavens, and liked simply the wind on her face, and being wholly alone, and the sense of pushing on a solid craft into soft-seeming darkness. When she slept it was with the rush of water in her ears, with the sense of currents parting around her, and sleep — such sound sleep — as the great, great heaviness of sea water descending.

There is a state of grace, she wrote in her notebook, in sleeping surrounded by withheld water.

One night, when the ship was becalmed on a plain of black, she saw silvery threads of light in a thin film on the surface of the ocean. They followed the pattern of waves and looked like fluctuating stripes, breaking, reshaping, breaking again, reshaping. A hemline in a dance. A ribbon dropped from a sky-gondola. A broken trace of moonbeam surfing the waves. Like and like and like and like: in truth it was like nothing she had ever seen before. It was of itself and radically particular.

"Bioluminescence," a voice somewhere said.

When Lucy turned to look, a little startled, she found a man standing close behind her, apparently peering at the ocean over her shoulder.

"Plankton, mostly. But underneath, down deep, there are fish that carry their own lights in spots on their cheeks, or in little pods dangling above their heads."

Bioluminescence: it was a wonderful word. It was a word that sounded as if it had travelled from the future, from a completely new knowledge, from a new dimension of scrutability.

"Sometimes," the stranger continued, "this shine is visible in decaying flesh or in plants; it's chemical, you know."

The man introduced himself as Captain William Crowley, lately in the service of the East India Company, now working for Her Majesty. He was returning home, he said.

It was too dark on the deck to see exactly what he looked

like, but Lucy was attracted to his voice and his tall upright shape. She wanted to pretend she was blind and reach out to touch him — as Mrs O'Connor assuredly would have done — so that she would sense by contour alone the face of this man who named things in the darkness.

"It's a hobby," he continued. "I'm interested in natural science. One day I hope to discover something, to have my name on a plant, or some half-invisible insect somewhere."

Lucy was not sure if the man was joking, but liked him immediately. Perhaps, indeed, she was seduced by him then, when he named a new light and stood obscured in shadow.

Captain William Crowley, having imparted his information, politely said goodnight and moved away, down the deck. It was only later, much later, that Lucy realised he had not bothered to ask her name, or wanted to discover anything about her.

They saw each other often after that, and William Crowley began to accompany Lucy on the deck at night. She learned he had been to England to deal with his older brother's estate, and to take over guardianship of his two small nieces. They were placed in a boarding school; their mother, who was distraught, he said, and overcome by grief, he had placed in an asylum. William related these things as though he had efficiently tidied up his family; "One must be decisive", he stated, "in matters emotional."

In her youthful inexperience Lucy saw no duplicity; she saw a novelistic captain, dashing and firm. When first he leaned forward to kiss her they were slipping past Africa, the ship tracing the outline of the great continent with slow fidelity to the coast, and it seemed fitting to the remote majesty of whatever lay before them that this man wanted to seal the occasion with a kiss. He slid his hand into the gaping placket of her skirt, and Lucy responded with grateful enthusiasm; she had waited for this touch, this confirmation, and for the fulfilment of the fiction she saw her life to be.

"Thank you," she said softly, rising from the kiss.

Retrospectively, perhaps, she invented their relationship. Perhaps she gave him symbols he was incapable of recognising. But the first time they lay together — this she knew for sure — they were rounding the famous Cape of Good Hope and she took the turmoil of the ocean as a kind of answering sign. The ship tossed and rolled and it seemed to Lucy that the world was reforming to match her new body. Waves crashed high against the ship and swept over the decks. The sea was thunderous. The air was stinging and alive. Lucy lay beside William Crowley, looking at his flushed cheeks and his nose and his closed tired eyes, and felt wide-awake and powerful enough to alter everything around her. Beneath the rough sheets she had discovered something remarkable: she had arrived *into* her own body. She understood now what might move a man to sail the sky for a woman, or cause a woman to track a man to the other side of the globe.

"Tell me more", Lucy whispered, "about bioluminescence."
She brushed strands of damp hair back from his forehead. William rolled away.

"You wouldn't understand," he said sleepily. "It's science, natural science."

So Lucy was left alone in the tossing dark.

"Please?" she said, sounding like a pleading child.

But William had begun snoring, or was pretending to snore. She longed to wake him to continue their unfinished conversation.

When they rose in the morning Lucy saw something she later read as ill-omen. On the deck a group of three gentlemen caught albatrosses with hooks and lines, pulling them screeching and crying from the open sky, and then gave them — five in all — to the assisting sailors. The sailors cut off the birds' feet, stuffed them with bran to begin a process of drying, then created from these grisly relics small purses and pouches for tobacco. Lucy refused one when it was offered. She thought of the birds' eerie squeals and their shocked dying eyes, glazed by betrayal.

30

DICKENS, GEORGE ELIOT, WILLIAM THACKERAY: LUCY DISCOVERED THE ship's small library. She thought for the first time about what it meant to read a novel. What process was this? What self-complication? What seance of other lives into her own imagination? Reading was this metaphysical meeting space — peculiar, specific, ardent, unusual — in which black words neatly spaced on a rectangular page persuaded her that hypothetical people were as real as she, that not diversion, but knowing, was the gift story gave her. She learnt how other people entered the adventure of being alive. She saw them move and think and make various choices. Rain fell, sun shone, journeys were undertaken. In a high window framed by billowy white curtains, a heroine blew kisses to her lover standing in shadows on the street, his face upturned to receive its inexpressible sensation; and in this moment, composed of alphabets, Lucy knew the shape of her own yearning. There were sight-lines, image tokens, between people and people, between people and objects and words on a page, that knitted the whole world in the purest geometry of connections. One simply had to notice. One had to remark.

Lucy fell backwards onto her bunk, and let her novel fold in her lap. The grains of the oak-wood above her appeared exquisite. There were knots, flaws, parallel lines. Lucy relaxed, and sighed, and closed her tired eyes.

Her mother's early stories flooded back to meet her. Lucy remembered oriental fantasies of dextrous artifice, fantasies of perished lovers and singular vehicles. She remembered the ice cave and a small girl learning to read. She remembered a tone of voice and the feminine scent of gardenia. It was like something swaying just in and out of vision — like light glancing in facets off ruffled water — a glimpse of herself, very tiny, as a six-year-old girl, nestled in a curve against Honoria's body.

This was memory as an asterix. The glory of the glimpse. The retrieval of just enough lit knowing to see her way forward.

"My mother used to tell me a story", Lucy began, "about a Flying Dutchman in India. He sailed the sky in a gondola suspended by a balloon, checking all the palaces in India for a beautiful princess."

William looked at Lucy, threw his head back, and laughed in a loud guffaw. "The Flying Dutchman in India," he exclaimed. "You certainly are original."

He could not be persuaded to explain the joke, nor did he wish to hear her mother's story.

The horizon was unhinging and sliding away. Lucy felt she was tilting into a kind of translucency. Her lover William Crowley could not quite see her. She was uncertain, sheer. She was the shape he entered, rocking her body, then departed too quickly, leaving the body-door ajar, leaving her feeling desolate and wide, wide open.

31

THE MORE LUCY KNEW WILLIAM'S BODY, THE MORE HE WITHDREW. The more she adored him, finding the crevice to kiss, learning the curve of his shoulder, tracing the line from nipple to nipple or the small dent in his chin, the more he grew silent and generally evasive. He stopped meeting her on the deck, so that she was obliged to knock on the door of his cabin and ask to be admitted. Sometimes he simply refused outright to see her, so she stood at his door, declaring girlish love, feeling herself conspicuous and deeply humiliated. Lucy overheard two sailors speaking about her and felt that she would collapse with shame. At card games she watched him and in the dining room she contrived to sit beside him, whether or not he deigned to talk. And then, capriciously, he would sometimes seize her, or take her by the wrist into his cabin, and undress her almost brutally. To say she was confused would be to discount the certainty of her feelings: Lucy desired William's presence, his caress, even his mocking laugh, more than she had desired anything before.

At some stage they fell into a kind of negotiated truce, and met with each other, prearranged, every second night. This relieved the sexual anxiety on both sides. William was more cordial and even at times happy. Lucy told him of Isaac Newton, the shining man in the box, and how she was sailing to meet him on a paid-for passage. Her lover was relieved and assured Lucy that the match was commonsensical and sound – a good fellow, well known, this Isaac Newton. William revealed he had a wife and four children waiting for him in Bombay. His father-in-law was wealthy, he said, and he would not jeopardise his fortune, nor his fine name. Lucy absorbed this information calmly. She realised he had assumed that she wished to claim him, when what she wished for was this dissolving of all her life into concentrated sensation, this extreme propinquity, and this perspective – resting her head sideways on his thin-haired chest – in which she discovered a silver scar and saw the very pores of his skin, in which the scented crust of dried sexual fluids, and the stain of her blood on the sheets, and the imprinted shape where the weight of two bodies lay, were the details of a hidden life she wanted uncovered. Along her arm were circular bruises where he had seized her too tightly: recording these marks in her notebook allowed Lucy to understand that such a grasp, on either side, is a kind of profanity, blemishing what it holds.

In *Great Expectations* Pip is in love with Estella, a woman incapable of returning, or even understanding, his feelings. This does not diminish his love, but renders it a form of despair, a strain in the throat, a slow *disheartening* as the heart remains unconfirmed. Lucy's remnant philosophies were all derived from fiction: she had no-one to whom she could confess, and could not write to her brother or uncle of what had occurred. How could she describe the changes wrought within her by unprecedented touch? William was smug and unworthy. But she was a young woman on a boat, a sixteen-year-old woman, floating towards a who-knows-what-destiny, presented as a daguerreotype in a velvet box. And she had collided and almost sunk in mid-ocean. She had collided with a physical enlivening she had until now only suspected.

If Lucy were to recover a *Special Thing Seen* from these meetings with a man who clearly did not love her, she would remember this: she had often been naked but for the locket that contained the silhouette of her mother, and one night, at last, he asked her what it was. She opened the Italian locket like a tiny book. When William glanced at the image he said casually: "She has your profile." No-one had commented before on any likeness Lucy shared with her mother. Lucy saw Honoria's face-shape as if for the first time. She was aware that her own face was cast in gold by the spermaceti candle that stood in a glass tube beside their bed, and in her fancy, at that instant, they were alchemically fused: she was the bright-lit original for her mother, the shadow.

That night, unaccountably, Lucy dreamed of her Ballarat cousin, Su-Lin. She dreamed she was married to Su-Lin and slept beside her — calmly, peacefully, not even needing to touch. Mrs McTierney appeared from nowhere and bent to kiss her on the cheek. In this dream Lucy was dimly aware of the sound of the ocean: she heard the soft continuous wash and mesh of the waves, their forming and unforming and their plash against the ship, as though the ocean itself constituted the knitted pattern of dreams.

32

HOW OFTEN, IN WHAT SMALL OR GIFTED OR IMPLAUSIBLE MOMENTS, do we replay what our parents knew, or did? How often do we feel — in another generation — what they imagined was sequestered in their own private skin? In its prismatic quality Bombay Harbour resembled Sydney Harbour, and Lucy could not have known that she experienced arrival as her mother did: with just the same arousal of spirit, with the same quickening of the heart, like a small fish leaping.

Lucy and William stood on the deck together as they entered Bombay Harbour. It was March and the light and heat were fierce. Lucy donned her sunhat and pulled down the veil to make a circle of semi-shade; William staunchly squinted into the sun and stood at attention. Around the ship moved dhows and fishing vessels of various types, with men in dhotis leaning on rudders or attending tattered sails; and beyond them were larger boats — merchant ships, a gunship, any number of imperial craft claiming the harbour. Lucy could see sailors of many nations and a group of Englishmen in uniform. There were numerous islands, it seemed, and the water was a magnificent indigo blue, a blue she would later, indelibly, associate with the Hindu god Krishna. On Victoria Dock carts and servants were obediently lining up; the men had red turbans and tight jackets and looked stifled in the heat. There were women in burqas and saris, and small boys carrying round metal panniers of food. At one end of the dock was a gilded tent, and there, roped off, Lucy could glimpse European women waiting together in a huddle, fanning their hot faces. Mixed-up syllables of women's words floated over the water. The air was aromatic: spiced food, cow dung, camphor, jasmine, and the sea air blowing up from Nariman Point, circulating in a briny whisk around the bay. Lucy breathed deeply: she wanted her body to fill entirely with all that her senses had given her. Through her veil the edge of India flared into existence.

At the side of the dock, Isaac Newton patiently waited. Lucy had worn, as instructed, a plum-coloured dress, so that he could easily distinguish her in the crowd, but in fact she was the only woman travelling alone and was thus clearly visible. She and William parted company with the briefest of words, and Lucy felt then the pang every mistress has felt – of returning a husband to his waiting family and standing apart, self-contained, without a touch or a kiss. She moved down the unsteady gangplank, clutching at the rope railing and fighting a powerful sensation of vertigo. Below her a gentleman, rather old-looking and moustacheless, waved shyly from a distance.

Isaac Newton was at least twenty years older than his daguerreotype suggested, but he was immediately solicitous and anxious to appear kind. Lucy raised her veil and inspected him obliquely: he looked like a man, she concluded, who was tired of life. His face was creased and his expression worn. He moved with an air of exhaustion and unconcern and looked at the world, off-centredly, through horn-rimmed glasses. To the left of her circle of vision Lucy could see William Crowley greet his family: he had a pretty plump wife and four look-alike daughters, as well as a huge entourage of attendants, servants, drivers and porters. He kissed his wife on the cheek, addressed his young children without bending down, and began at once barking orders about his voluminous luggage. His manner was brusque and rude, and he did not, not once, glance in Lucy's direction. He had already forgotten her.

"Just one piece of luggage?" Isaac Newton enquired.

Lucy saw that he had knobbly, arthritic-looking hands. He seemed to tremble.

For both of them matters practical made their meeting easier. Lucy was excited, but tired. She felt queasy in the heat and unsure of how to respond to this gentleman beside her. William's voice rose up; he was shouting at someone. His face looked sneering, granite-hard and unfamiliar. Isaac took Lucy by the elbow and guided her to a painted yellow carriage. She was pleased to subside into its shade and its hollow seclusion.

If she remembers little of that first ride away from the dock, it is perhaps because she was preoccupied with her departed lover and because there were too many new visions to absorb. Isaac sat stiffly opposite, peering over his glasses, silent, openly curious, and Lucy looked out the window to avoid his gaze. She knew at once that this world had a denser pigmentation: colours were brighter, more strident, and more adhesive to their objects. After Australia, Lucy had considered England a pale and etiolated nation, full of slightly pinched and death-white faces; but India surely outshone Australia; its palette was that from which others derived. In the streets there were rickshaws, push-trolleys and horse-drawn tongas, as well as pedestrians, traders, beggars, holy men, shoppers, bullocks, fleet children who ran shouting alongside their carriage; and all bore colour remarkably, as if they met the tough specifications of another order of being.

It is like sexual hunger, Lucy thought, to wish always to see things like this, to see more intensely, more zealously, more unrealistically. To wish everything into a state of stunning exaggeration.

Looking enchanted her. When did she first realise? That even one empty street held an aurora of light. That the delectable visibility of things was her aim and her vocation.

33

ISAAC LIVED IN AN AREA OF BOMBAY KNOWN AS MALABAR HILL. It was a wealthy European enclave, full of spacious and sprawling colonial houses. His own, perched high, had an expansive view of the Arabian Sea. Banyan and tamarind trees surrounded the house and there was a sloping shady garden of tropical flowers. The shade was pure lapis lazuli, the shadows perfumed and cavernous.

Within the house were many artifacts Isaac had collected on his travels. Statuettes, wall hangings, embroideries, religious icons, musical instruments. By the front doorway there was a particularly beautiful limestone head of Buddha; he had a topknot and a small spot at the centre of his forehead, and he was smiling, with his two eyes softly closed.

"My cabinet of curiosities," Isaac announced when they first entered the house. He was proud of his collection. He spoke, he said, Murathi, Hindi, Gujarati, Sidi and Urdu, and knew intimately the history and provenance of every object he possessed.

"I'm not really English any more," he added, sounding pleased with himself. It was a peculiar introduction, as though issued in warning.

Servants appeared before them and lined up for inspection: there were three women and three men and a boy who looked about twelve. All greeted Lucy by holding their palms together, in the neat shape of a temple. She felt honoured and nodded to each in turn. Isaac named only the oldest servant – Asok – a man with a red-henna beard and a stiff tall posture.

"My retainer," he said, "for almost thirty years." The young boy was a punkah-wallah: his job was to pull the cord of an overhead fan, shaped like a miniature curtain.

"And what is your name?" Lucy bent to ask.

The boy smiled shyly, said nothing, and quickly averted his eyes. He had smallpox scars on his cheeks and a look of discomfort. Later, as Lucy sat awkwardly with Isaac, drinking tea, she became aware of the thick frills of the punkah fan swishing softly above her. She could see that they were manipulated by a rope that stretched outside, to the verandah. The faint creaking of a pulley and the swish-swish sound ever after signified her unease with the orders of labour and leisure.

Swish-swish; swish-swish: a susurration in the air, a fan-sound amplified. It was like the unquiet and restless whisper of the dead.

Their sleeping quarters were separate and side by side. At night Lucy could hear Isaac washing, undressing and preparing for bed, and wondered at his body naked, at his body aroused, at what, after all, might yet happen between them. Sometimes she glimpsed him in stripes through a gap in the teak planks of the wall: he was slim and boyish, his body almost feminine, and he hummed to himself as he moved about his room. She could not imagine ever making love to this man. She could not, she reflected, imagine herself as his wife.

Yet Lucy tried hard to imagine this Isaac Newton. In the house his body became articulate and his manner easier; he relaxed in familiar clutter and among his extraordinary objects. With the servants he was distant, hieratic, but was given to tender exclamations over small works of craft, and the pertinent quotation of lines of poetry. He had regard for cracks along the side of an old pot, but was uninterested in the lives of those who orbited around him. Altogether more complex than William Crowley, he was also, in some ways, much more remote, used to his own complete and solitary-seeming dominion. One day, not long after arrival in the house, Lucy startled him while he was busy combing his hair. He turned surprised and with a look of violation, holding the comb raised like a sword above his head. In the mirror it reduplicated; he was posed as a kind of oriental warrior. Lucy learned to keep her distance, to take her time.

Standing before the life-sized head of the Buddha, Lucy asked: "Why has he such long ears?"

"The elongated lobes", Isaac answered, pleased at her question, "are a reminder of his life as a prince, when he wore pendant earrings. Before Enlightenment, that is. Before he became the Buddha."

"And why are his eyes closed?" Lucy continued.

"Because", Isaac said patiently, "he doesn't need to see. He doesn't need to see what you and I see."

This was to be their principal form of communication: Lucy's ignorant questions, Isaac's learned responses. She pondered what might be known without being seen. She pondered the way the body carries small signatures of its former selves. Small telltale markings.

Lucy's life entered a period of containment and suspension. She trailed around the house, feeling ill-at-ease and hypocritical. On every shelf and in every corner there were exquisite Indian objects, still, secretive things, silent and precious, but Lucy longed for chatter and touch and human communion. The servants retreated as she drew near and Isaac spent whole days alone in his study, translating, apparently, a government document. ("My civilising purpose", he called his work.) Lucy marvelled that he had learned so many languages but seemed without fellow feeling for the people who spoke them: whenever he commented on the "natives", as he called them, he was invariably critical. Neither spoke of the pretext of her visit, nor of her uncle, Neville, nor of how they should get to know each other. Isaac lived in a kind of distended time; his sense of duration, Lucy was sure, was entirely different to hers. Time stretched in an endless repetition of the tinkle of brass bells to summon chai, or to take tiffin, or to have some small ministration performed by the gentle brown hands he resolutely, stubbornly, failed to appreciate. Isaac lived a life of physical inactivity: he barely moved from his desk and was set there, in a kind of tortoiseshell light from the shadow of leaves cast on a damp tatty screen, an immobile, self-satisfied emblem of privilege. His shape above the desk was a human comma: everything about him *paused*.

At length it was her body, her woman's body, that altered irrevocably the relations between them. That gave Lucy back to herself with affirmation and delight.

At first she was somewhat alarmed and fearful. Lucy had learned from the women in the factory the symptoms of pregnancy so when she felt nausea in the morning she knew at once that a child was forming in her unmarried womb. As she retched into a basin held by a woman she would later know as Bashanti, she could see in the eyes of the servant that everyone else in the household, everyone but Isaac, also knew what indisposed her and what wracked her body every morning. In her sour mouth potential lies began to shape; she rehearsed shrewd alibis and exonerations – pirates perhaps, or sailors, had attacked her – but knew that in the end she would tell the truth. The women at the factory had also discussed the means of disposing of pregnancy − hot gin, violent exercise, crawling upstairs backwards − but Lucy felt that this state had been given to her out of a passion she could not wish undone or revoked. She would greet her pregnancy in a rapture of confident serenity. She would live, she resolved, wholly and indivisibly, not splitting herself off from any category of experience.

At nights, in the room Isaac Newton had set aside for her, filled with large-bloomed cut flowers and lacy Madras curtains, behind which swam a square of moonlit Arabian sea, Lucy thought principally of William Crowley. It was not only the pleasure of congress she imagined − his weight pressing into her, his gasps, and her own − but she remembered a particular, almost fugitive, moment after their lovemaking, a moment of dressing. She had noticed the vulnerable area at the back of his thighs − it was a pale screen of skin, petal-looking in texture − and it seemed a testimony of the most intimate lover's knowledge. He was not the uniformed, confident, hale-and-hearty fellow, but a man who carried, as it were, the flag of his own childhood. And though she knew now of his definitive meanness and duplicity, she wanted to preserve him thus, in continuity with this quality of unremarked softness. She was, even now, even with him returned irretrievably to his prestigious family, conscious that his beguiling physical beauty inhered in just such contradictions.

Lucy and Isaac were having dinner, separated by a row of tallow candles set in ceramic figures. Above, on the ceiling, Lucy could see lizards the colour of human skin and with peculiar little hands, hanging upside down, their thin necks arched. They made odd tongue-clicking sounds, like an old woman, disapproving. Halfway through her reverie, Isaac leaned across the table.

"You have something to tell me, I believe?"

Lucy caught his gaze and saw that it was blurry and elegiac; Isaac adjusted his eyeglasses in a self-conscious gesture.

"How did you know?"

"My servant, Asok. I would have preferred to hear it from you."

Lucy was silent. Isaac waited for a few seconds before going on.

"Was it William Crowley? I saw you standing together on the ship. He has an utterly caddish reputation."

What could Lucy say? That he knew a new word for light? That he taught her the shock of sensation? That she did not regret, in any way, their volatile passage together? There is a vain and private dimension to having seen one's moisture glisten on the surface of another's body. It is inimical to words. It is untranslatable.

Lucy stared down at her plate of fiery, half-eaten food.

"Well?"

"Forgive me, Isaac, I have nothing to say."

"Ah!"

Isaac was a gentleman; he would not pursue the matter. But he felt embarrassed and put-upon, and inwardly cursed Neville Brady, who in his letter had promised a mature woman of thirty, chaste and well educated. A governess, he had written, a governess, chaste and well educated, as in a Brontë novel.

They resumed their dinner in strenuous silence. Asok entered, padding around the table in soft blue slippers. He glanced knowingly at Lucy, replaced a sputtering candle, then left with discretion. Lucy thought again of the distinctive tortoiseshell light that fixed Isaac like a statue each day at his desk: its amber seal somehow removed him from all that she treasured, from her rocking body and from other bodies, from the world in which vessels strain against the weight of the sea, and from the perilous possibility of incarnations by touch.

"I wonder", said Lucy, wishing to change the subject, "if you can tell me the story of the Flying Dutchman of India."

Across the dinner table small insects were diving at the candles, extinguishing themselves in a crazy second.

34

ASOK PADDED PAST AGAIN, HIS HENNA BEARD BLAZING IN THE candle-light. He took with him a handful of dirty dishes.

"Someone has misled or fooled you," Isaac pronounced. "There is a fable, and there is an opera, but neither, I assure you, is in any way Indian. Someone else has taken advantage of your sweet gullibility."

Lucy decided to ignore this comment, which seemed contrived to hurt.

"Tell me, then," she said, "what I ought to know."

Isaac raised a glass of wine. He liked nothing better than to be consulted for his knowledge. His appearance became temporarily cheerful.

"The story begins", he said in a school-masterish tone, "in 1641. A Dutch sea captain, a Captain van der Decken, is sailing home to Holland from the Dutch East Indies. (Indies: perhaps this is where your misconstrual comes in.) As he rounds the Cape of Good Hope, a fierce storm arises. Dark clouds gather, his crew screams in terror, and the ship hits a rock and begins to sink. The Dutchman, furious and railing against his fate, shouts a pledge to the heavens that he *will* round the Cape, even if it takes until the end of time. Thereafter he is doomed to sail in a phantom ship throughout eternity, although one day each seven years he may set foot on dry land and seek redemption through a woman's love."

"Is he?" Lucy asked. "Is he redeemed?"

"I'm not really sure. In the Wagner opera, which he wrote, I think, in 1843, the whole point is that his redemption both succeeds and fails. As I understand it . . ."

(Here Isaac sounded uncertain.)

"One day the Dutchman, on land at last, meets another sea captain, Daland, and offers him great wealth for lodging for one night. Seeing a business opportunity, as it were, Captain Daland takes the Dutchman home, where his daughter Senta has been singing about her fantasy love for a Dutchman."

Lucy's eyebrows raised.

"You must remember, my dear, that the story is a fable. And that opera is even more unreal and fabulous."

"In any case," he resumed, "Senta has known all her life that she will save the Dutchman, and has dreamed beforehand that her father will bring home a mysterious lover."

"And?" Lucy asked.

"Well, of course they are betrothed, more or less immediately, and the fated match is duly accomplished. However," – and here Isaac paused for special effect – "there is another man, Erik, who is in love with Senta. He follows her, and the Dutchman, seeing them together, believes that Senta has been unfaithful, so he leaves. Senta protests her love, but the Dutchman releases her from her vow, setting her free. As he boards his ship once again, Senta throws herself into the ocean. The ship finally sinks, and the lovers go down together in a locked embrace. And that's it. That's the end. *Finis*."

Lucy fiddled with her fork and looked dissatisfied.

"Is there a light in this story?" she asked. "A special light?"

"A light? I suppose you mean the famous red glow. The phantom ship emits an eerie red light, and some sailors superstitiously believe that the ship is still visible today during storms off the Cape. Whoever actually sights the ship, however, will die a horrible death."

"And is there a gondola suspended from a balloon?"

"Goodness, no," said Isaac emphatically. "There is no gondola. No balloon."

"And does Senta bear a distingushing birthmark?"

"I have told you", said Isaac, trying hard to sound patient, "all that I know."

He took a last gulp of his wine and rose abruptly.

"I feel like a prisoner," Lucy blurted out.

Isaac stopped in his tracks. He looked shocked and dismayed.

"We will discuss your grievances tomorrow," he said in a haltering voice. "Now I bid you goodnight."

It was like a scene in a novel. Lucy saw how melodramatically they confronted each other. How stale their words were.

Isaac almost rushed for the door and Lucy remained at the table. She rested her hands protectively across her controversial belly. Salty wind blew in from Arabia. The night was fierce, inclement. Yet another tale of a sacrificial woman. Of ghosts. Grand passions. Extravagant double-deaths. What am I doing here? she asked herself.

Later that night, way past midnight, she rose and moved to the open window. The wind was rising and carried with it a distant sound of the ocean. There was a scent of rain and distant lightning, flashing. If she leaned beyond the window it might begin raining, and the rain would then wet her tired face, and she would shine against this dense Indian darkness before her.

Now, just this humid swaddling air.

Lucy remembered her mother lying very still on a long wicker chair, her pregnant belly huge and her skin livid. She was fanning herself, just before her death. The wave of a duck-egg blue fan, patterned with chrysanthemums: this small detail retained, held close, held in mournful embrace, so that her ever-fading mother would not completely disappear.

Senta: the name returned. Then Lucy began to weep: who was she weeping for?

35

PERHAPS IT IS THE OPACITY, NOT THE TRANSPARENCY, OF OTHERS THAT one finds compelling. Beyond the face is a funnel to hidden selves, intact qualities one doesn't expect, the mysteries secreted in dim and blessed moments, the store of memories, unbeheld, that only a single person knows. Scraps of sure self. Fragments of undeveloped character. Wounds. Recoveries. Innermost otherness. So Lucy began at length to reconsider Isaac Newton, and to find in him a kind of emotional gravity.

They grew at first to tolerate and then even to like each other. The agreement was that Lucy would stay in the house and bear the child, and then, when it was strong enough, together return to England under the name of Newton. This would preserve both her dignity and his, Isaac said, and no-one in the Old Country ever need know the true circumstances of paternity. In the meantime, they should "make the most of it": he would try to know her, more openly, and she would be at liberty to leave the house and make small excursions – accompanied by himself or a by servant – into the city and to outlying areas. He offered his knobbly hand and they shook heartily, as men do, but Lucy noticed too the beginnings of a palsied tremor. The quake of mortality. The quiver of death deep inside the tendons of the body. It was the first time since the day of her arrival that he had actually touched her, and she thought of Grandpa James at the coach siding, jerkily waving.

There were places Lucy would travel to where her own ignorance astounded her. She entered customs and buildings she knew nothing about. People around her spoke and she understood not a single word. She considered herself a crude cipher of the West, carrying her own culture as impeding knowledge. This territory she had entered was on the whole indifferent to her presence, and might well engulf or erase the speck of empire she accidentally represented. It was in the marketplace, where foreign women were never seen, that she felt most keenly her presumptuous misplacement. Local women of exceptional beauty brushed and slid alongside: she thought her own clothes a stiff and ridiculous dome against their fluent forms and loose clinging fabrics. She was, more-over, pastel to their augmented hues; she had never before felt so bleached and so encased. There were merchants standing behind pyramids of many-coloured spices who hailed her and smiled; they waved their hands like magicians over their mini-geographies, enticing the stranger to inspect and buy. Lucy instructed Bashanti to acquire a few ounces of turmeric, for no reason other than its colour, and that it was something she could confidently name. There were men in saffron robes devoted to multiform gods, and children with kohl around their eyes and small grasping hands. There were beggars with damaged limbs and whole families with fingers and faces eroded by leprosy. Lucy asked Bashanti to give them money, but her servant simply flung coins in their general direction, afraid of their touch. Flowers garlanded tiny shrines in nooks and crannies, and sewage and rubbish lay strewn beneath her feet. So many people and so prepossessed.

Lucy would have liked to announce that she was Australian, not English, but she knew that here the distinction was probably meaningless. Her face was a white lamp in a sea of brass. She wished herself dark. She wished herself Indian, part of this throng of purposeful, myth-saturated, interconnected people. Now and then she passed another foreigner, a man, inevitably, who would nod, or touch the rim of his hat, as if exchanging secret English messages in code. Lucy had no wish to communicate with these other lamps who felt – she could tell – that they shone more brightly and more importantly than anyone else, that they dispensed white light with a civil-ising purpose. In her imagination she flickered in the midst of the crowd, her face appearing here and there, inconstant and impermanent, a kind of fleeting figment, in a more general and self-sufficient sea of brown. Only once did she see William Crowley's face in the distance, half-shaded under an awning, partially averted, and her heart jolted and her pulse quick-ened. When he saw her and realised who she was, he turned quickly into an alley. Coward, Lucy thought. Yet she felt – she had to admit it – annoyed at her own excitation.

For all his self-enclosure, Isaac Newton was impressed with Lucy Strange and her spirited assertions. She had no interest in the various English women's social clubs, of bridge or badminton, of chit-chat or church talk, but befriended the servants, salaamed complete strangers, made trips to the Persian bazaar, where no foreign-born woman would dare be seen, and regarded everything with a wide-awake and intentioned gaze. He had seen her pause at a market stall just to lean over and breathe in its scent; he had seen her cry out with tears in her eyes, coming unexpectedly upon a small statue of Lakshmi, decorated with strings of yellow roses and orange marigolds. Bashanti, who understood but could not (or would not) speak English, clearly adored her, and even Asok seemed to watch her with untypical interest. She had changed the very space and dimensions of his house: everyone was conscious of her presence as if she was a human magnet pulling at their faces; everyone orientated their perceptions around her. He discovered Lucy patiently teaching Asok the game of chess, and not long after, braiding Bashanti's long black hair, with no notion at all that a memsahib does not – should not – perform such mundane and rank-breaking acts. More than this, Isaac suspected Lucy of "native appetites": she met the world with a distinctly impassioned sensuality.

This image, above all: Lucy had bought kohl at the market and ringed her eyes, so that they suddenly appeared enlarged and nocturnal. Isaac had come upon her reading and her startled face lifted, and there, over-defined, were two sooty pools. Sensing she had surprised him more than he had surprised her, Lucy raised her hands in a conciliatory prayer-shape:

"*Namaste,*" she said.

Then she resumed her reading, unaware of the extent of her provocation. Australians, Isaac told himself, had no sense of decorum. Her eyes looked barbarian; her eyes looked primitive.

Isaac Newton was a man who lived with secrets. Two, in particular. The first was that he had once been in love with Neville Brady. They became friends in Calcutta, not long after Neville first arrived, and Isaac found him charming, sensitive, good-natured and comical. He learnt early on that his companion was more or less a compulsive liar, but saw this as an extension of his love of story and his impulse to entertaining fabulation. In those early years Neville was also dissolute and philandering, so the friends fell out over his visits to nautches and prostitutes. Isaac threatened more than once to have nothing more to do with him, but always relented. He realised he was in love when Neville succumbed to simultaneous bouts of malaria and syphilis. Isaac dabbed his brow, fed him quinine and magnesia, and applied mercury ointment to sores on his penis, while Neville joked about his condition and was by turns irritable, anecdotal and deadly quiet: he performed a range of selves Isaac had never before witnessed in another man. The act of nursing was the act that enjoined them. During the illness Isaac realised what it was that he felt. That he would have been shattered, destroyed, if Neville had not recovered.

His second secret he thought he might one day tell Lucy. He would tell her about seeing a production of *The Flying Dutchman*, long ago, in the city of Frankfurt, as a young traveller on his very first visit to the Continent. He was twenty-two years old – and still an Englishman – yet he wept out loud in the auditorium when Senta and the Dutchman sunk together under the waves. The music rose, there was a dramatic red light pulsing, and his heart burst open. He had to bury his face in his hands so that no-one would see his hot tears. It was the first and last time Isaac Newton had ever shamed himself thus in public. And he had waited all his life to tell someone about it.

36

WHAT REMADE HER WORLD: THE CAPTURE OF LIGHT.

For Lucy the photography studio was a revelation. Mr Victor Browne, a man with a bleary vague manner and large clumsy hands, practised a focused, crisp and careful art. Isaac had decided that he and Lucy should have a portrait photograph taken, before — as he so indelicately put it — her shape betrayed her, an image, he said, that would help later on and might even serve as consolation to the future child. This reasoning defeated Lucy, but she acquiesced, keen to see what she looked like halted in a lens, and keen too to see the rooms in which such portraits were produced. Victor Browne ushered them into his little world of props and false objects. There were painted screens, one a scene of the Taj Mahal, one a *trompe l'oeil* drawing room, another a leafy park-scape with French lamps and a curved path, and pretend objects — a marble pillar that was in fact made of painted wood, and a stuffed monkey, looking animated, on an ornate perch. There was a furled parasol for ladies to hold and a teak chair for gentlemen to sit on. Lucy spotted a pile of albumen paper and smiled to herself. The tissue of times past. The shell cracked open.

Part of the ceiling had been removed so that the studio was open to the sky and bright. Victor fussed around, moving this or that object, shifting or settling, lowering or raising his camera stand. He was particularly concerned, he said, with shadows which appeared every day at this time, for only half an hour or so, cast by trees outside the window onto the interior wall. The shadows were like blossoms; Lucy saw them as powdery blue against the white screen of the wall. Victor's intention was the eradication of the blossom and the production of a uniform unshadowed backdrop, against which the odd couple might be immaculately posed. He moved them to the far left of his viewing frame, just outside the reach of shadow, and there he arrested them: Isaac in the chair, stiffly serious, his hands on his knees, his knuckles polished-looking like large white beads, and Lucy standing behind and to the right, bemused and excited.

Bad timing, pronounced Victor, referring to the shadows, from under a dark cloth. He held up a device which exploded in a muffled puff. Light flashed across the room, filling to the brim Lucy's wide, newly photographic eyes.

The image Victor Browne created posed Isaac Newton and Lucy Strange as a legitimately married couple in an English park. The power of the flash had removed some of Isaac's years; he looked both younger and more solid than he appeared in real life; Lucy, on the other hand, appeared older and less substantial. Since she was superstitious it seemed plausible that the rumour was true: that the camera removed some human quotient or iota with each image it took. Later, indeed, Lucy will worry that her portraits, silver and gold and sometimes resembling icons, have filched spirit-stuff or soul-stuff in the instant of registration. Later, Lucy stared narcissistically at Victor Browne's photograph, but found no pool of portrait beauty over which to linger and transform. She saw herself, over all, as plain and severe. She wondered if others looked at her face and saw this plain severe woman, older than her years and in a state of paranormal fade and recession. All she could think of was this: *People will look at this image when I am dead; it will*

stand in for me, for ever, just as my mother's austere paper cut-out — all stasis
and reduction — now cruelly betokens her.

It was her destiny, this visit.

Lucy persuaded Isaac to let her learn the art of photography. Victor Browne would instruct her, and during the time of pregnancy she would be occupied in this not-too-unladylike fashion. Isaac was amused and interested and agreed to pay Mr Browne a small weekly sum to instruct Lucy in what he joked was a devilish art. Lucy watched the two shake hands. Isaac's handshake was uncharacteristically firm; it seemed to belong to another man.

Under the nocturnal shadow of the velvet drape, through the frame, and the lens, and the aperture, and the glass, that together directed her vision into this specialised seeing, Lucy discovered the machine that is a gift-boxed tribute to the eye. She looked as she never had, imagining a picture frame or a box that isolated the continuous and unceasing flux of things into clear aesthetic units, into achieved moments of observation. Where Victor sedated and mortified all that he saw — his box, thought Lucy, functioned as a seeing-eye coffin — she imagined a mobile apparatus, one that travelled everywhere with her and that discerned the capability of all things, all ordinary things, to be seen singly and remarkably. Chemicals, glass, mechanical reproduction — these combined to make Lucy feel entirely modern, a woman of the future. She loved even the sharp acidic smell of the fixing agent, that permeated the studio, omnipresently, like industrial perfume.

Lucy's understanding made sense of her book of *Special Things Seen*: somehow — was it possible? — she had always been a photographer. Lucy tried to discuss this supposition with Victor Browne, but he looked sceptical and wry.

"This is science," said Victor, "not prettified seeing. It is pure calculation."

Victor had wiry red hair and a kind tone to his voice. He was not like William, and not like Isaac, who carried their authority in forms of knowledge; instead he believed himself the fallible end of a system of strictly estimable decisions. He was the humble hand that covered the lens and sank the paper into its bath of glistening silver nitrate.

"Do you think", persisted Lucy, "that we shall one day, far in the future, have the means to capture in a photograph the exact colour of your hair?"

Victor turned to Lucy, looking embarrassed.

"Certainly not," he said. "Colour is God's business."

For Victor photography was purely fake – vain posturings; the stiff fictions of a happy marriage, placement in other, more remote and more comfortable worlds. For Lucy it was a shift in time itself, and a celebration of the lit-up gaze. The imposture of studio work did not really trouble her: she knew it was one mode among many of the concentrated image. There were still moments in time, moments arcane, seductive, trivial, breathtaking, that waited for the sidelong glance, the split-second of notice, the opening up of an irrefutable and auratic presence. She had always known this. She had always believed this to be so. She had always been, after all, a photographer.

The holy man:

At the door of a temple sat a holy man, a sadhu, with his foot tied to his neck. His forced-up leg was withered and odd-angled – it looked no longer human – and his body was thin and appeared like walnut wood. He had long hair and a matted beard and a single shred of rag around his waist. Lucy bent before the holy man and filled his bowl with money. The man smiled. His eyes shone. His eyes were the only part of him that seemed still to have the capacity to be fully flexible and alive.

Lucy caught his gaze directly: Yes, she thought, just as my eyes make this man a spectacle, his return to me a refusal, and a claim of humanity.

Arre! he called out.

The elephant:

It was in the *Bombay Gazette*: Mayhem at Chowpatty. An elephant had run amok, killing five people including his mahout, and trampling numerous small dwellings and market stalls. Members of the local constabulary had tracked and shot it, blasting the crazed elephant brains to spattered mush. After the initial sensational story, there were letters to the paper about the non-removal of the carcass: it stank, it was unsightly, it was publicly decaying. Lucy set off with Bashanti to see the dead elephant.

Who could have thought so much flesh was contained in one being? The massive creature lay on its side, its head thrown back. The tusks had been hacked off, and so had the feet, so that there were bloody exposed areas swarming with insects. The stench was foul. A poor fellow in a ragged turban stood guard over the elephant; he scratched unselfconsciously at his genitals and exchanged a few words with Bashanti, clearly curious that she had brought her memsahib to this dreadful site. Lucy picked out the word *farangi*, foreigner, one of the few she knew well. Bashanti lowered her voice and turned away and Lucy tried to imagine what explanation she might be inventing.

Lucy had come to witness bioluminescence. If there is light visible in posthumous flesh, she reasoned, then it will be visible on this scale, with this mountainous beast. She moved foward to the creature, holding her nose to suppress nausea, and saw all of a sudden the flesh disturbed, as though the animal still pulsed and was still, despite its disfiguring mutilation, alive. Lucy's heart bucked and shuddered and she instinctively stepped back, then saw two rats leaving the carcass through one of the open legs. There was no shine but that of viscera; there was nothing lovely or bright. There was no redeeming conversion of death into luminescent surface. It was only a mass of putrescence, a butchered mess.

That night Lucy dreamed that she set up a camera in front of the elephant. When she looked through the viewfinder she saw right into its body, right into the red heart, which still beat feebly and bore a glazed and delicate shine. As she took the photograph, the elephant rose on its bloody stumps and shuffled away. This was not a nightmare; it was the artful conversion Lucy had hoped in waking life to see.

The pan-wallah:

He sat cross-legged on the ground before a wood plank platform upon which rested, neatly stacked, his bundles of pan leaves bound around mixtures of tobacco, spices and herbs. For a few paise clients bought this unusual confection and headed off, chewing vigorously, filling their cheeks with complicated, explosive tastes. The pan-wallah advertised his wares by his own perpetual chewing. He favoured betel nut, and every minute or so spat a gob of bright crimson fluid onto the ground around him. It was a forest of peonies. Lucy noticed the floral composition of betel stains that circled the pan-wallah. He was at the centre of a kind of artwork. He was in a pattern of spat fluid.

"Disgusting, isn't it," Isaac had whispered at her side.

"Sometimes," he added, ever the teacher, "there are special pan mixtures that include gold dust or silver paste. For the wealthy, you understand.

Lucy loved this idea: chewing on gold and treating it as mere food or condiment. "I want to try some," she whispered back to Isaac, and felt him immediately recoil.

Later, when in secret Lucy had persuaded Bashanti to bring her a sample of pan, she sat chewing the tough leaves and attending to the pan-effects. Her mouth burnt, tingled, was becoming numb, and began to fill up with curious liquids. She spat onto the floor and saw before her a small mound of gleaming brownish muck.

The widows:

A sanitary detachment from the army was spraying tenements with limewash to protect against bubonic plague. The air was filled with caustic stink and people rushed past, and ducked into doorways, complaining. Lucy saw a group of widows, four women – only one grey-haired – hurry past the sanitary operation in their white mourning saris, and she decided, since Bashanti was buying cloth, to slip away and follow. The four women turned into a side street and visited a stall that sold puja items, items for worship, then moved in single file into a hidden-away temple.

The temple space was dim and filled with incense. It took a minute or so for Lucy's eyes to adjust to the darkness, but there they were, the four women, just a few steps in front of her. Each sounded a hanging bell as they entered the temple and moved forward without speaking. They placed their items – a few old apples, rice, jasmine and bilwa flowers – at the foot of a statue of Ganesha, the elephant-headed god. Ganesha was luridly plump and jolly, with a sweetmeat in his hand and a single rat beneath his foot: he appeared to be dancing. Saffron powder and sandal paste smeared his face and he bore supernumerous garlands of bright yellow marigolds. The women prayed, waving smoke over their faces with slow fluent gestures. Lucy felt again oversized in her stiff-domed skirt, which caught and snagged against the rough stone walls of the temple. Her pregnant body was too full for these narrow spaces. There was chanting, more prayers, and more dense threads of incense. A holy man in a corner saw Lucy and gestured, but she had no idea what he was communicating. She was not sure why she had come, or if her presence was sacrilegious. She watched the widows – who throughout their ceremony had not noticed her at all – they appeared as lineaments of female shape in the claustrophobic dark. The single woman with grey hair seemed to be the only completed stripe: Lucy was tethered to her image. She was a completed pillar of white in the dark, dark temple.

"I've been thinking", said Lucy, "about Victor Browne's photograph."

Isaac looked up from the book he was reading.

"The shadows," she continued. "I think it would have been more interesting with the blossom-looking shadows."

Isaac now enjoyed their quirky conversations.

"You want the maculate, not the immaculate," he responded. "*Maculare*: spotted, stained, blemished. Not *immaculate*, like the holy virgin."

"Yes," said Lucy. "The world is like this, don't you think? Marked, and shadowed, and flecked with time."

Isaac sat back in his chair. *Flecked with time.* He still could see only a slight indication of Lucy's pregnancy and wondered vaguely if she was mistaken, if they could start again. She reminded him in some ways of her uncle, Neville Brady. Families contain peculiar routes of similitude and dissimilitude. He remembered Neville in Calcutta, all those years ago, stuffing his mouth with sugared fennel seeds then leaning forward – with a most alarming presumption and intimacy – so that Isaac could smell the crushed seeds and his sweet aniseed breath. Isaac had looked into the mouth of Neville Brady and glimpsed there a rare physical confidence that he thought at the time was specifically Australian. And he had experienced at that moment a sexual shudder.

"Flecked," he repeated. "That is it, exactly. Nothing in my cabinet of curiosities is without fleck."

It was some time later, when Lucy had become a photographer herself, that she considered again, and more critically, the spectacle of the dead elephant and her own credulity. Vision included these ghastly moments and fearful contaminations. In India she had seen things she wished instantly to forget, things that rose up to the eyes with unmediated power. Violations. Deaths. Sufferings exceeding any image. She was ashamed at the vulgarity of her wish to beautify. How, she wondered silently, to attest it all? All the lights, all the darks, all the blotted cloudings in between.

37

Dearest Lucy,

It seems such a long time since you left and Neville and I both miss you terribly. We received your news with some dismay, but are pleased that Mr Newton has made sensible arrangements after the confinement for your return to England. You draw a veil over the details — perhaps it is shame or distress that quietens your pen — but if you should decide to tell of the events on that disastrous ship, and if you should ever wish to identify the fellow who robbed you of your innocence, I shall listen with loving compassion and take action as appropriate or necessary. I can never forgive myself for not accompanying you on the passage to India, and ask you, dear sister, to one day pardon my mistake. Enough said, for the moment, on this difficult topic, but know that both I and Neville are concerned fundamentally for your precious well-being, and long to have you returned to us safely and in good health.

My work at the Childish Establishment continues to flourish. Mr Childe has kindly taken me under his wing, as they say, and taught me the trade of magic-lantern operator. I can set slides, work the lamps, and direct musicians and narrators. Recently we showed a series of scenes from Shakespeare, and I thought of you, dear sister, when the ghost scene from Hamlet arrived. Mr Childe had arranged for a puff of smoke and a cymbal clap to accompany the ghost's appearance (the slide itself was a little disappointing — clearly a man enshrouded in a sheet), but a woman in the front row rose up, screamed, and then collapsed *in a faint. This event caused a sensation. I could not help thinking: partickler when she see the ghost!*

My good fortune continues: I made the acquaintance of the faint young woman, who turns out to be exactly my age and employed in the City as a teacher of pianoforte. Her name is Violet Weller and I believe — though I have told no-one and can barely believe I am disclosing it to you — that we may, God-willing, have a future together. She is sweet and intelligent and shares my love of the phantasmagoria, to which she has often come (although, to be truthful, I had not noticed her presence before). Violet lives with her parents — whom I've yet to meet — somewhere in Kentish Town.

Uncle Neville continues to search for our mother and has found a new medium, one he considers superior to Madame d'Esperance. The new woman, Madame Noir, is dark and possibly gypsy, and Neville believes that this alone recommends her and makes her more spiritually competent. So far our ectoplasmic mother has predicted your safe return with a healthy son, and Neville is much heartened by this news and mentions it frequently. He hopes, I cautiously add, the infant might be named for him.

Neville has found some irregular work at an importers' warehouse in the docklands where, luck of luck, he works with Indian products and is again immersed in the world of his beloved spices. He brings home samples for me to try, but I cannot abide the tastes. When you return, Neville says, he shall cook an Indian curry in celebration, and he will supply the proper ingredients in the proper proportions!

Neville's health, I must confess, is not the best. He looks old and ruddy and has a shortness of breath and pains in the chest, for which he takes a noxious-looking tincture, supplied by Madame Noir. It has yet to prove an efficient remedy, and I fear it represents another dimension of his too-trusting nature. He also calls out at night, and is troubled by bad dreams, but says that — thankfully — since I began working the lanterns my sleepwalking has ceased. My own health is robust — touch wood — I have none of those spasms of coughing you witnessed before you left. Violet told me I looked "in the pink" of health, which I took to be a compliment and evidence of her growing affection towards me.

Neville says to send you his love and requests that you seek "native" advice for the time of birth. He claims the Indians have a secret system of healing over four thousand years old and that it is based on the body's composition of energies of earth, fire and wind. The fire sign, he says, is connected to a kind of bodily light, which he claims must be regulated in the act of birth. (He also told me that my sleepwalking was a disorder of wind!) I have no notion of the veracity of this information or the soundness of the advice, but promised Uncle Neville I would pass it on.

We await your return anxiously and with much loving eagerness. Travel safely, dear sister, and guard your own new light carefully.

Your ever-loving brother,
Thomas

38

IT WAS IN THE FIFTH MONTH OF HER PREGNANCY, WHEN LUCY SHOWED, even then, only a small mound of belly, that she travelled with Isaac to the island of Elephanta. In the Bombay Harbour, a few miles from the city, rested an immense temple complex, carved of rock, and dedicated to the three-faced god, Shiva. Isaac said it was one site he hoped they would visit together. On the ferry, they rode comfortably in each other's company. Lucy felt exulted to be once again on the water. The world before her was like blown glass: some fluid shape expanding, sphere-wise and breathful, into a glistening new form, some sense of the weird plausibility of transmogrification. The wind was high and the broad boat rocked and tossed. Lucy saw Isaac seize the railing and vomit into the heaving ocean. She turned her face into full sunshine and full wind, held on to her bonnet, and smiled. Fishermen, *kolis*, squatted confidently on the prows of their small wooden craft, received and answered her waves, surprised, perhaps, at this foreigner's bold and out-of-the-ordinary friendliness. She would have liked to call out a greeting in their language, but realised, with a shock of shame, that she knew no kind hallos and no grateful expressions. So she placed her hands in a temple shape and bowed in their direction.

They disembarked on a small beach, at which an old woman

in a brown sari sold lotus-seed rosaries, and had a long climb, up stone steps, to the Elephanta Cave. Isaac chattered like Baedeker: "This island was named by the Portuguese", he declared, "for an elephant statue that resided here, at the beach. It was moved away in 1814. The Portuguese – vile desecrators – defaced many of the carvings, but what you will see is still remarkable . . . finished somewhere between 450 and 750 AD . . . carved directly into stone, a huge effort, incredibly significant . . ."

He puffed as he spoke. Lucy surged up the steps towards the temple, hoping to leave him behind and to recover her own quiet thoughts; but then took pity on Isaac and waited, looking down on his hatted head, feeling unaccustomed affection, taking his trembly hand at the very top of the steps.

Before her were massive stone columns at the main entrance to the temple, which was composed of shrines, aisles, courtyards and porticos.

"It was designed in a great mandala," Isaac said, "to accommodate a circumambulatory ritual that involved observance of images dedicated to the god Shiva. Energy", he added enigmatically, "is the purpose of this shape."

Inside was chill, damp and mysterious. Lucy clutched Isaac's hand and felt a squeeze of acknowledgement. They were friends, after all. They stood side by side in the sacred shadows.

The most beautiful statue was the Trimurti, the triple-headed god, tall, calm and resting with eyes closed. Lucy had seen many representations of Shiva in Bombay, but this grey basalt figure, dignified and elaborate, seemed to her the most compelling. There were scenes too of Shiva myths – his wedding with Parvati, his impaling of the demon of darkness on a trident, his emerging from a mountain and holding back the waters of the Ganges; there was even the remains of the dancing Shiva, the Nataraj, Isaac called it, with his extra arms and his leg raised, dancing in a halo of fire. At the centre of the temple was an abstract shape, long, pure, resting in a circular receptacle. It dripped water and was smeared with sandalwood paste. Flowers and bel leaves draped and adorned its borders.

Lucy looked across at Isaac, silently questioning. He cleared his throat and nervously adjusted his cravat.

"It's the male organ," Isaac said. "The Shiva lingam. Fertility. Another image, you might say, of the divinity of Shiva. There are also female organs that serve for worship."

Lucy paused. She felt perplexed, dumb, enshrined in her own cramped circle of questions. What did she know? She knew that there were images, things seen, imperative as desire; that there were stories in images and the theft of essences in photographs; that myths were remade in stained glass and cast in bronze and stone, and that in the midst of all these verifying representations, she was a creature of half-belief, or no-belief, for whom all these mysteries were garbled, or blank, or intractably mistranslated.

Isaac looked wan and drawn. The short voyage and the climb up the stone stairs had exhausted him. But Lucy felt her own vigour converging as questions converged.

"Like the crucifix, this simplicity?"

"Well, yes," Isaac hesitated, "except that this symbolism is of course sexual, not deathly."

"Sexual not deathly," she repeated, to Isaac's embarrassment.

Isaac looked down at his English shoes.

"There are many kinds of shrine, then?"

"Yes," he confirmed. "There are many, many kinds of shrine."

Is the camera a shrine?

Later, as Lucy made her way, much too quickly, back down

the stairs to the water, she thought, as she stepped, of the human eye — pupil, lens, crystalline humour. Then she thought of the camera, the extension of her eye, the black-magic box of secluded light, the black box of recorded and refracted information, of objects inverted, of death defeated. She thought too of the glass plates that held the envisioned world — in eight by ten inches — returned to itself, as an act — surely — as an act of devotion. Lucy halted on the steps to look back at Isaac, above and behind her. He was a thin struggling shape. He gave a feeble wave. Called out something. Hurried up. Reached for his hat. Again she stopped and waited, overcome with sympathetic affection, consenting, in her own way, to let him join her.

At the beach, Lucy purchased a rosary of lotus seeds. This signified no sudden accession of piety, but simple concern for the old woman in the worn brown sari who stood there in the heat, looking impoverished and desperate for a sale. On the water, once again, she turned her face to the sun. The ocean was lustrous, glaring, a vast fluid light, round as an eyeball and puckered in the still-rising wind.

There are many, many kinds of shrine.

39

IT WAS, THEY AGREED, LIKE A BRIEF FORM OF MARRIAGE. IN THE LAST few months of her pregnancy, Isaac and Lucy behaved as man and wife; they slept in the same bed and kissed goodnight, they offered up verbal intimacies and cared for each other, even though both knew of their inevitable parting. It was a pretence that afforded each a temporary rescue from loneliness and the exchange of whispered secrets deep in the night. It was tender and richly embraced – not merely convenient – and both behaved towards the other with poise and respect. Isaac told Lucy of his occasion of weeping at the Frankfurt performance of *The Flying Dutchman*, and she evinced no surprise, but congratulated him on the candour of his youthful response. Later, emboldened, and much to his own surprise, he told her he had been in love with her uncle, Neville – *enamoured* was the word he actually used – that he had been demented with desire and sick with lust. Lucy tried to imagine Uncle Neville so wholly attractive, but somehow could not; yet she was moved by the trust implicit in Isaac's confession. In return Lucy told Isaac of her parents' deaths, of the arrival of Neville in Australia and the trip to England. She described the albumen factory, and spoke at length on her theories of photographic seeing. She did not speak – not ever – of William Crowley, nor did she mention her *Special Things Seen*.

The stories they exchanged threaded the gulf of night, years, nations and experience, lacing them close. They lay in the high tapering cone of a mosquito net, chatting in random, sincere disclosures. When asked about his faith Isaac declared he was atheist: he believed gods were the imaginative projection of human qualities and adventures. Lucy agreed. "But this did not diminish", Isaac added, "the art achievements of sacred expression that seemed in themselves, and of themselves, tran-scendental . . . Mystery inheres only in art," Isaac said firmly.

Lucy had rejoined with the obvious question: "But what is art?"

One day Lucy had been out, on an excursion with Bashanti, when they witnessed an accident. A man was scaling a build-ing, carrying a large mirror, when he lost his footing and fell to the ground. Since he did not release the mirror it shattered into his body as he landed; a long spear of glass entered his chest and another cut an artery in his arm. Blood spurted everywhere and the man died almost instantly. He was young and rather handsome, lying in the shiny mess with his dead eyes open and his turban undone. A curious crowd gathered, murmuring their shock, and Bashanti began weeping quietly into her dupatta. What in retrospect disturbed Lucy was her fascination. She stared fixedly at the scene: the angled spears of mirror reflecting the gathering crowd; crows flying upwards from a tamarind in a spray of black shapes; the woman in a blue sari who leaned forward to seek a pulse in the dead man's neck, then retreated, her garment stained with blood. The mirror and the blood were an irresistible combination. Lucy could not help herself; she thought of repetition; she thought of a photograph.

Two men came and carted the body away in a sling of cloth. A rickshaw wallah loaded the larger pieces of glass onto his rickshaw, and children were collecting hand-sized shards and small dangerous fragments. Within a few minutes there was only a field of drying blood, sprinkled with sparkles of shattered mirror. *Blood in bucketsful.*

At the scene Lucy was in a state of cataleptic calm, but later found herself trembling, as her grandfather and Isaac trembled. There were many deaths in India — everyone knew this — but death by mirror seemed to her particularly meaningless, the counter-logic to finding one's own face, there, alive, as one dressed, or admired oneself, or leaned forward critically or vainly to examine a feature. Lucy did not speak of the accident to Isaac (it seemed so private, like another special thing seen), but found herself rising up at night, in a kind of delayed shock, seeing again the full details of the improbable accident, arrayed before her like an awful apparition. There was the mystery of art, but there was also this mystery, the slash of mortality, the strange mingled order and disorder of death, death which happened, and then returned, in its own numinous glow.

Lucy could not record or exorcise the death by mirror. She stored it as a secret, as an untaken photograph. She carried now a great sense of the inadvertent brutality of life. After their act of witness Lucy had enfolded Bashanti in her arms, mutely comforting, and then they left together, in a hurry, immediately to return home. Later they drank tea and ate milk sweets flavoured with cardamom. They sat beside each other, almost touching, on a patterned rug on the floor. Lucy brushed and braided Bashanti's hair and placed within it a circle of new frangipani blossoms. Their perfume was glorious. It was a tiny communion against all the possibilities of disaster and accident.

"Lucy?" Isaac called softly. His voice floated on the night.

The name returned her to the bedroom, to the bed they shared, to the things here, around her, on this particular night. As if her own name — of course — was a small flare of light.

40

SHE LAY WITH HER EYES CLOSED, LOOKING INWARD, LIKE AN INDIAN god. Her hands were knitted over her belly, which was now a sturdy globe, and she had become a kind of global traveller. In her meditation she saw the slow-spinning planet, memorised, as from childhood, according to continents, seas, nations, capital cities; there was corpulent Australia, removed and remote, there were the marine-looking archipelagoes of Southeast Asia (looking like coral, like sea cucumbers, like beaded strings of seaweed); there was the planchette of India, and the Arabian Sea, and there, further on, was the proud body shape of Africa. Upwards – since her route was cursive, perverse and driven by mind-winds – lay lumpish Western Europe, studded with important names, the finicky jagged outlines of the United Kingdom, the feline swallowing shapes of Scandinavia. She zigzagged backwards to move over Russia and China, and settled somewhere in Japan, the site for any number of exotic dreams and conclusions, chosen for the incomparable beauty of its shape. The entire continent of America did not figure on this journey; Lucy's globe placed the Arabian Sea at the centre, and regarded itineraries and destinations by the illogical attractions of shapes.

Her own shape was troubling. Her body quaked and rumbled. She wondered briefly if her flightiness was some infantile regression, occasioned by the upheavals of her double anatomy, or if indeed she simply needed to counter in light-headed fantasy the inordinate heaviness that encumbered her every movement in the world. As her body had grown the pregnancy seemed more and more monumental; her belly was like St Paul's, like the Taj Mahal, an alabaster dome held up by the gaping architecture of her slim pelvic bone. Bashanti rubbed Lucy with fragrant obstetric oils but still she did not humanise. Her skin looked like polished blue-and-white marble and the baby remained a wholly unimaginable inhabitant, curled like the ammonite in quartz pointed out to Lucy as a child. It was difficult to imagine this tight form movable or uncurled. How could she possibly be large enough? She might crack open, or even die. Lucy was tormented by fearful dreams of her mother's last pregnancy: the high mound of her body, the rose blush of her death, the ruination of her husband, glimpsed, in every dream, standing somewhere in the distance in his dirty pyjamas. The past returned disarranged and symbolic, destroying years of practised forget-fulness in sudden, fevered visions.

One night Lucy had a nightmare about her eyes expanding. To match the size of her body, her eyeballs grew and grew, so that she was deformed and saw everything with alarming magnification. At first this was a kind of pleasant surprise, like discovering a new or superhuman skill, but then the world loomed over and crowded her; everything achieved a monstrous proximity and definition. She woke with a start, crying out loud, her hands clasped over her eyes as if to hold them in.

Lucy heard Isaac rouse in the bed beside her.

"My Taj, my belly," she explained. "Giving me nightmares again."

Isaac rolled over.

"Don't call it that, please."

He was silent for a moment, then drowsily went on:

"The Taj Mahal was a tomb. Shah Jahan built it for his wife, Mumtaz Mahal, after she died giving birth to their fourteenth child."

"You're superstitious?"

"Only in certain things. Naming, for example. Those of us without faith have the compensations of superstition."

Lucy was silent.

Isaac stretched over and touched her cheek.

"It will be all right," he said tenderly. "I promise, it will be all right. Neville will be a father, after all."

"Fourteen," Lucy said, "imagine that."

But she was thinking still of Isaac's enigmatic words: *Neville will be a father, after all.*

The birth coincided with a celebration, since Lucy's ninth month was also the month of Diwali, the Festival of Lights. All over the city lit earthenware lamps, diyas, were arranged around doorways and windows and in neat rows along pathways, to welcome home from exile the mythical king Rama and his wife Sita; more particularly it was a time for welcoming Lakshmi, the goddess of Wealth and Good Fortune. She was one of those voluptuous goddesses, always depicted dressed in a red sari, with lavish gold ornaments, cushiony lotus flowers and sometimes with two friendly elephants, spraying arcs of water. Isaac had been obliged to buy the servants new clothes; Lucy watched Bashanti, dressed in a lovely new garment, woven with beiges and pinks, set forth small rows of diyas along the windowsill and the path leading up to the front doorway. She presented prasad, sweetmeats, at their family shrine and everyone in the house was newly bathed and looking festive. The women had flowers in their hair; Asok had his beard freshly hennaed.

On the night of the birth there were lanterns and fireworks everywhere. Isaac and Lucy had been out walking when the labour began; perhaps the noise of the fireworks, Lucy thought, had disturbed her baby into action. She saw the night blaze up in florid explosions, but felt suddenly blackened by pain and unable to support her own weight. Her knees folded and buckled and she collapsed forward, onto her stomach. Lucy was dimly aware that Isaac was calling out in panic – waving his arms in *farangi* abandon – but she was already transported somewhere and sometime else, conscious that fluid had gushed between her legs, enthralled by the imperative nature of her own body, curious, entirely curious, to know what would happen next. A cart arrived and she felt her heavy body hauled up; and then, in a miraculous ebbing, she was just as before, still and alert.

"It's stopped," she reassured Isaac. "Just for the moment."

Lucy could smell pungent firework smoke and the bullock pulling the cart. She saw the driver turn around at the sound of her voice. Sweat ran down the front of her gown and covered her face and she wiped herself, without thinking, with the hem of her skirt. The air rang with distant chanting and drumming and the clash of cymbals.

"At last, it's happening. At last," she said.

The cart took them back through streets they had earlier walked, back past all the pools of illumination set forth for kings and goddesses, back past light after light after light after light. Lucy's eyes were wide and starry.

"Auspicious," whispered Isaac, "highly auspicious."

He had taken her sweaty hand and held it between his thighs.

Later she will move again beyond his reach, and enter the dilations and contractions of time and space itself. There was a violence to birth; no-one had told her that. None of the women in the albumen factory had mentioned this strange battering sorrow, this engulfing sadness as the body at last expels what it has grown.

An English doctor had been summoned. From her bed Lucy could see him out of the corner of her eye, resting in Isaac's favourite armchair, smoking a cigar, which he waved like a conductor's baton as he spoke. The punkah fan swished in the air above his head, driven by the invisible pock-marked boy.

"We just have to wait," the doctor told Isaac. He had a pencil moustache and a haughty manner, and Lucy disliked him immediately. She called for Bashanti, but for her pains was left alone. At some stage Isaac poked his head around the door. His face was flushed and anxious, his eyes enormous.

"We just have to wait," he said nervously, echoing the doctor's words.

Then he disappeared.

Lucy began travelling. She flew again over the familiar shapes of the globe, noting landforms and waterways, naming oceans and mountain ranges and capital cities. This time she explored both North and South America, skimming along what she imagined was the route of the Amazon. Brazil, she remembered, was Thomas's own reverie, so she halted there awhile, thinking of her brother. The wind and the sun were in her face and she felt joyful and illimitable, swinging through space like that, like a woman of the future.

The night stilled and the oil lamps finally began to extinguish. A gentle wind from the ocean scattered the embers of dying bonfires in brief bright spurts. In the early hours of the morning Bombay was settling to sleep, subsiding into slow-motioned pyrotechnical dreams. When the baby was at last delivered Lucy didn't know where or when she was: as her dome collapsed the span of her planetary vision also collapsed, and she felt as if she had entered a new, redeemed time and a new, close focus. Lucy saw her daughter lifted upside-down before her, the umbilical cord asway, the shape still partially unfurled. She was glazed with vernix and blood-smear and was a sign, a wonder. She was irrefutable, glistening, a kind of absolute light.

PART THREE

"It is not merely the likeness which is precious . . . but the association, and the sense of nearness involved in the thing . . . the fact of the *very shadow of the person* lying there fixed for ever!"

Elizabeth Barrett Browning, on the daguerreotype

41

THE DAY LUCY AND HER DAUGHTER LEFT INDIA A THUNDERSTORM
rolled in across the harbour. There was a low smothering
sky and a sense of cloudburst anticipation, and everything
drooped under immense monsoonal humidity. Hibiscus
flowers inclined like melancholy faces. Insects sounded
mournful and full of complaint. The inanimate world was
registering a kind of depression. In the house lay the additional
weight of incommunicable feeling. Isaac was restless and
unhappy; the servants fussed and kept entering and leaving
rooms for no reason.

Early that morning Lucy had given everyone gifts. To each
of the servants, a small prettily decorated envelope of money,
and collectively a photograph she had taken months earlier. It
was an image of all of them together, standing in full sunshine
in the back garden, in front of their quarters. They were
delighted at her gift and giggled and exclaimed, pointing at
themselves and making amused jests. Later, more privately,
Lucy gave Bashanti a gold bracelet she had seen her admire
(and for which she had to borrow money from Isaac), and Asok
a chess-set, carved in onyx and jade, (which had, to her surprise,
been ridiculously cheap). Bashanti wept and Asok bowed. Lucy
wanted to express gratitude for all they had given her, but was
limited to a few phrases of child-level Gujarati. She salaamed

repeatedly, offering a gesture in the place of language. To Isaac Lucy gave a small brass Nataraj, found in the market. It was not rare, or expensive, or a collector's item, but seemed to her both the typical and singular symbol of their short time together. Isaac accepted the common object with grace and good humour. In return he gave Lucy a painted miniature, depicting the popular god Krishna and his consort Radha. Krishna was a blue-skinned lover in proud profile, standing outside in a garden, and Radha waited inside a kind of silky fringed tent, wearing a fine drifting garment which exposed her skin. Details were picked out in paisley-shapes of gold leaf, in the most exacting handiwork. On Radha's chest lay two iridescent blue wings: she had willed her heart to grow wings, Isaac explained, so that it could fly from the tent and see her lover. These were fashioned with real beetle wings, cut precisely to shape and carefully pasted in place. Lucy leaned her face to Radha's breast to double-check the substance of the wings.

"Bioluminescence?" Lucy had asked.

The eroticism of Isaac's gift surprised her. He had seemed so physically placid and inert she wondered, at one stage, whether he had any sexual experience at all. He had occasionally kissed her goodnight, but his touch had been, for the most part, occasional and hesitant. The image she held in her hands seemed freighted with the passion he wished to express.

Now she was on the ship, at the railing, and Bombay was shrinking in the distance. On the dock, she had watched Isaac battle to withhold his feelings, humiliated by his own emotional excess.

"The *Dutchman* effect," he joked rather feebly.

He blew his nose loudly on a monogrammed handkerchief, and tried to recompose himself by tugging at his cuffs and turning his hat by the rim.

His hands trembled in a way that filled Lucy with pity.

"Foolishness," Isaac said, trying to explain away his feelings.

Lucy kissed Isaac on the cheek and promised that she would one day return, when baby Ellen was a girl, when Ellen was grown, so that he could see what had become of them and how their histories had unfolded.

"You won't return," Isaac stated, just under his breath.

He blew his nose again; his misery was dreadful to witness. Lucy thought he sounded like a wounded or petulant child, and only later, much later, knew that his prediction was true.

As the city receded the stormy dark skies split open. Rain fell in weighty slant-wise sheets, obliterating last glimpses of the Indian shoreline. The waves were choppy and agitated. Briny air in swift currents blew around the ship.

For now she retreated to her cabin, dragging her heavy splashed skirt and holding her small baby close. The air was a physical manifestation of tearful departure. It was crowded with clamour, smells and uncontrollable effects. People fled, looking dashed and damaged, or frowned at the sky from under canvas shelters, or wiped their wet faces and brushed back damp strands of hair, resentful of dishevelment and the intercession of large forces.

"Fookin' rain," she heard a sailor exclaim. As though he had been personally insulted by the weather.

Against the authority of the world and its dramas, against Isaac, ships, journeys, sky, Lucy set in focus her insubordinate preoccupation with her child. In this vessel of iron and wood, built sturdily in defiance of the ocean itself, she lay on the creaking cabin bunk and gazed, wholly besotted, at her small rocking daughter.

Ellen was four months old and still startled by the dazzling novelty of the world. She looked at faces as if they appeared in a flash of lightning before her, and slept twitching and whimpering, still communing with images, still responding to all she had incomprehensibly and vividly seen. When Lucy rose up at night to feed her, fighting through exhaustion and the fuzzy density of being half-awake, she was often confronted by Ellen's steady, wide-awake gaze, looking up at her, directly, in the wavering oil-lamplight. At the breast Ellen played with her mother's locket as she drank, leaned backwards for a rest, flinging out her arm, and then leaned forwards and drank again, never once breaking the compelling circuit of their gaze. She was complete and individual. A new set of eyes in the world. A new shining face.

Perhaps, Lucy thought, every parent feels this, the awe of so delicate, so partial, a connection. This belief that the curve of an infant's head is the loveliest thing ever to have existed. That the scent of breast milk is sweetly incomparable. That touch has never before been so fine. The earlobe. The eyelid. The pulsing fontanelle. Perhaps this is the most ordinary experience of all. Perhaps it has always been thus. Ellen's breath was a miracle. The weight of her small shape in the middle of the night was a gift. The budded mouth, the mobile expressions, the curled and uncurled hands, these were what Uncle Neville would call a New Beginning; these were what, in her sleepiness, isolation and unmarried-mother-shame, she realised was the rhapsodic element she had sometimes seen in a glance through the viewfinder − the swift intimation of unrealised beauty, the shaft of brightness unaccounted for, the revelatory outline.

In the peculiar duration of early maternity and with the slow flight of time on a long sea voyage, Lucy thought at length about what had been given to her to see. When, late at night, after feeding and settling Ellen, she looked again at the miniature painting that Isaac had given her, she felt she had achieved a small degree of understanding. She held the image to the light, and rubbed the beetle wings with her thumb, gently testing their texture. The word was bioluminescence. There was in every living thing this elusive capacity. In lovers. In the newborn. In the congregation at a temple. In the man who was killed by a mirror and lay on his back looking at death. Every person was a lighthouse, a signal of presence. This was nothing sentimental: it was the single, wise thing that she utterly knew. It was the knowledge that would carry her through a night of deathly terror – when the ship pitched fearfully, the timbers groaned, objects shattered everywhere and dangerously flew, manly sailors wept with fear and called out to Heaven – to the surprising egg-yellow of a dawn becalmed.

42

THE RETURN WAS A DISTURBING CONFLUENCE OF SYSTEMS OF doubling and subtraction.

Thomas was waiting at the dock with his friend, Violet Weller. They stood together, the same height, the same age, the same physical colouring, and the same open, honest, lovable faces. Lucy thought they could easily have been mistaken for twins. Thomas embraced his sister heartily, holding her as if he hadn't really believed she'd return, and Violet held Ellen on her hip, exactly as Lucy liked to hold her, exclaiming at her beauty, bending towards her like a mother.

"Neville?" Lucy asked.

"Neville died," Thomas said softly. "Only two weeks ago. An accident. A ghastly accident."

His voice petered and seized.

Later, after dinner, Thomas took Lucy into the garden and with moonshine on his face and a voice husky with pain told her the bare circumstances of Neville's death. Then, in a small act of self-protection, he told her at much greater length of Charles Dickens' death in June, of how he had stood in a line with thousands of others filing into Westminster Abbey, and felt the dignity of the occasion, and its ceremony, and its historical importance.

"The woman in front of me", he said distractedly, "carried

a single stalk of white rose tied with a rag; she must have been at least seventy years old." Something in this detail caused Thomas to pause. Two stripes of tears, the slick patina of moonlight, like trails of absence. And in the air a revenant sound: swish-swish, swish-swish.

43

THOMAS AND VIOLET WERE MARRIED WITHIN A MONTH OF LUCY'S return. There was a small ceremony at St Giles, attended only by Violet's parents, Max and Matilda, and Lucy and Ellen. Outside the church they all gathered, radiant together, under a soft fleecy sky, beaming at anyone or anything that happened to pass by. Pigeons sprayed upwards in an audible surge. There were broad waves, well-wishings, the doffing of a top hat. Violet held a posy of snowdrops and fishfern and Thomas wore one of Neville's old Indian scarves. Later Lucy posed the couple at Mr and Mrs Weller's house, and photographed them, now looking much more subdued, beside a gigantic brass urn and a rather striking floral arrangement of jagged red tulips. As she peered at her brother and his twinlike wife, Lucy noticed how the spirit on the church steps had entirely dissolved, how this false composure and formal arrangement had leached their jubilation. So many wedding photographs, she predicted, would be exactly like this, stolid, anaemic, respectable, dull. Figures in a formal, stiff relation. Yet the couple was thrilled that Lucy was an amateur photographer, and patiently arranged and rearranged themselves for her glassy stare. They struck various poses, the last one comical, with Violet pretending to leap on Thomas with cat's claws, and Thomas cowering beneath her, his hands open in alarm. (It was something, they said later, they had seen in a magic-lantern show, some kind of private joke.)

As an afterthought Lucy asked for one last photograph: an image *maculate*, she announced. She moved the newlyweds to the back doorway so that they stood within a strong, specific frame and leaf-shadow across their faces showed them riddled with light. She stared at them staring back. They were trying hard not to blink or squint in the unseasonably sharp light. Lucy's hands became heavy. Her heart swelled with love.

With her head there, under the cover, she was hidden but not disassociated. She saw them link arms. Heard wingbeat high behind her. A whispered remark from Max. A "shoosh" from Matilda. Somewhere too, there was Ellen, gurgling in her perambulator, looking up at the sky. It was as if, for a second, evanescent time settled down. As if the glass lens, apt and uncomplicated, saw for her and for all time complete testimony of that moment.

"Thank you," she said, as she emerged from the hood.

Violet performed a neat curtsy; she was full of play.

Over brandy and wedding cake, Max and Matilda Weller expressed concern at Lucy's recent bereavement — her being so young, and with a bairn, and so brave to float all that way across the ocean — and she realised that Thomas had told them she was a widow. The Wellers were too polite to enquire what poor Mr Newton had died of, but Lucy reminded herself she must ask her brother what story was abroad. Both Violet's parents seemed much older than Lucy had expected, and she learned later that her sister-in-law had been adopted from a foundling home at the age of five. The three shared an idiosyncratic culture of wordplays and jokes, and Violet often took her aged parents with her to the magic-lantern shows. They were, Lucy thought, like a family out of Dickens: Max had a bent grizzled friendliness and cutaway mittens which he waved as he spoke; Matilda was pert, birdlike and wore old-fashioned pink bonnets that emphasised the flush jolliness and roundness of her face. Max Weller had been a watchmaker, and all around the parlour stood clocks of many eras, shapes and kinds, some half-disembowelled, their brass innards gleaming. They were all firmly stopped. Matilda couldn't bear, she explained, the false liveliness of clocks, the sound of all that incessant tick-tocking and chiming.

Violet Strange moved in with Thomas, Lucy and the baby, and from the beginning her marriage was a state of effusion. She even enjoyed her new name. "They were all strangers," she said, "and yet they were unestranged. They were the strangest family in London and would produce strange, strange children."

Since Thomas and Lucy had thought of their name only with a kind of habitual and vague disparagement, Violet's invigorated delight struck them as both enchanting and curious.

("She married you for your name," Lucy whispered to Thomas, and he tilted his head and heartily laughed.)

In bed at night, feeding Ellen as quietly as she could, Lucy could hear the intimate noises of Thomas and Violet talking together. The specific tone of their talk was that of voices given to each other, with pure relief, in new-found community.

It was a world now of small rooms, a commanding baby, and a bride who joked and cooked and planted little vases of violets ("so that you won't forget who I am!") in every corner of their cosy dwelling. Lucy understood that both Thomas and Violet had a dimension of joy, of keenness-to-life, that she did not seem to possess. She admired the loving play between them and felt a little jealous; the air around the newlyweds was charged with sexual anticipation and neither Thomas nor Violet could pass each other in a room without in some way brushing skin, or clothes, or offering inaudible words of endearment. Thomas had possessed a collection of snakeskins when he was a child: why does Lucy remember this now? There were three, in fact. He kept them in a box, revealing them on special occasions, and with inordinate pride. One by one he would hold them up like streamers, and they would dangle and sway fraily, strips of diamond or zigzag, finely woven sheaths, still magically intact after life departed. He guarded each snakeskin as if it was a talisman of secret knowledge. Now, watching Thomas and Violet prepare a meal together, cutting up meat and vegetables for Irish stew, talking softly in sing-song voices, with their heads inclined in each other's direction, she thought again for some reason of the three papery skins her brother once kept in a box under his bed. Thomas had shed skins many more times than she. Thomas had been reborn into this contented husband who no longer sleep-walked, or was afraid of ghosts, or flinched at his own reflection arising suddenly, revocably, in the bathroom mirror. He was renewed, younger looking, his happiness evident.

Later Lucy would look at the wedding prints, as they glided in luminous fluid, surfacing to definition. Photography had given her second sight. She saw Thomas and Violet again, amorous, manifest. She had by magic and illusion travelled them through time, made them ever-alive, endowed their faces with the nacre of wet seashells and the promise of persisting youthfully, on their marriage day, for generations to come.

"Behold me," each face called from the past to the future.

44

AS WELL AS *SPECIAL THINGS SEEN*, LUCY INCLUDED IN THE TITLE TO her diary *Photographs Not Taken*. This way, she reasoned, she could include in her reckoning those things she had seen photographically but without her camera, those things that moved her, with or without a frame, and those things she had not seen physically, but been granted vision of, by others. There was a whole fugitive empire of images to which she felt affinity and loyalty. Her diary would compel attentiveness. Would claim these images. Would set her formally agape.

The bath:

She had asked Thomas to bathe Ellen and he had been reluctant. When she placed the naked baby into his large hands he became awkward and self-conscious, holding his niece at a distance from his body, unable to relax. Ellen, by contrast, looked compliant and peaceful. Her plump rosy body was cool and musk-scented and she moved her arms in wide circles as if she was already a swimmer.

Lucy set the tin bath of tepid water on the kitchen table before Thomas and he lowered the baby. She watched as by degrees his body began to discover the fluidity of the act. With his left hand Thomas held Ellen behind her back and with his right he began gently to splash and clean her, wiping the folds under her chin, sweeping his palm over her scalp, brushing with water her plump arms and her lizard-shaped belly. Ellen held up her hand to be grasped, and Thomas allowed his finger to be taken in her tiny fist. At this point he looked up at his watching sister. His face was joyful. He looked proud and aglow.

The fireworks factory:

In the month before Ellen was born, Lucy had been on an excursion alone, seeking gifts. She had wandered into an unknown part of the city and quickly become lost. At every turn, people seemed to point or stare at her; she felt absurd, haphazard; she could feel sweat on her face and a panicky acceleration racing in her pulse. Her large pregnant belly was impossibly heavy.

A beggar's thin arm reached out and dragged at Lucy's skirt, catching like a claw, and she pulled away roughly and turned into a doorway. Inside was like a heated cave. There was a bitter stinging stench of sulphur and magnesium and in the dim light Lucy could see twenty or so boys, all no older than twelve, squatting on the floor in cramped groups making bundles of firecrackers. They mixed and rolled the toxic powder and stuffed tubes of cardboard with their thin skilled fingers. Even in the half-light she could see that many had been burned, and that the group of boys closest to the doorway, stamping paper with a red Ganesha and packing crackers in rows, all had missing digits, or in some cases, missing hands. One of the boys waved his stump arm at her and shouted something that made all the other boys laugh. Lucy saw his fierceness, his mockery, his wish to strike her where she stood. She hitched her heavy skirts, turned and fled. The boy's face had been lovely: it was still the face of a child, but anguished with the need for an explanation for the sacrifice of his hand.

During the time of Diwali, during the pains that caused her to fall forward in the street at night as the sky flashed and boomed and reconstellated with fireworks, this boy's expression floated back to her like an accusation.

The kiss:

She had come upon them kissing. Violet was leaning her back on the hallway wall and Thomas was facing her. With both arms he enclosed her in the brackets of his body and pressed with the slight possessive tilt of his hips. A bluebell-shaped light hung above them, like a singular star.

They were rapt and isolated. They were on their own planet. Lucy stood guiltily watching the full length of the kiss; it was a long intake of breath, nothing like the rough quick kisses of William Crowley. She stepped backwards – just in time – so that the couple could preserve their aloof orbit of just two. In a likeness that made their kiss appear heraldic.

The earth:

As they grew to know each other, Lucy and Violet began to talk and exchange stories.

"What do you remember", Lucy had asked, "of the Grosvenor Foundling Home?" Violet remembered the pungent smell of floor polish and the feel of a rough flaxen garment rubbing across her skin. She remembered the taste of gruel flavoured with salt and lumps of turnip, and the experience of being pinched on the arm, again and again, by an older child.

"Images," Lucy persisted. "What images do you remember?"

Violet paused, then said she remembered nothing much but the rather ordinary image of a graveyard. It was beside the building – far too close for emotional comfort – and she could see thin whitewashed wooden crosses – thin as children's bodies – from the perpendicular window on the staircase. When there was a scarlet-fever epidemic children began to disappear and the earth in the graveyard became newly churned and dark. For a long time there were no new crosses, but then one day, suddenly, they all appeared together: seven, she remembered. Seven new crosses.

"Like Lowood School? Like the school in *Jane Eyre*?"

Violet confessed she had never read the novel *Jane Eyre*. She apologised for the scant, ordinary quality of her images and the dispersed and simplistic nature of her memories. She said later that she had wanted to say something that would impress her new sister – to describe some airy beam of light resting on a single cross, its shadow, its promise, its everlasting etc., but could manufacture nothing beyond churned earth and the certainty of seven lost souls.

Neville:

This much Thomas imparted: the death was a foolish accident.

Neville had been to see Madame Noir and was returning by way of the public house to tell his good news. At the Spread Eagle he had been in particularly fine form:

he talked excitedly, his beery cheeks burning with liquor, of the predicted destiny of his grandchild, Neville Newton. The boy would be a genius with numbers and enter the World of Commerce, Madame Noir had foretold. He had Great Expectations: he would make a fortune by the time he was eighteen years old.

The publican said later that Neville's happiness was clear; he talked fondly of the child's father, the late-lamented Mr Newton, whom he had known as a companion in Bombay, India, and said he would soon bring the child to the Spread Eagle — the epiphany, he said — for all to see.

Lucy envisioned him, flushed and voluble, among rows of glittering glass and cynical patrons. ("Neville will be a father, after all.") He leaned on the bar, his dirty scarf dangling, his elbows crooked like a child at a pantomime, inventing futures. His charming smile flooded the room with a good-humoured glow, so that the other men forgave him his fatuous tales, and played along, indulging him, feeling their own hidden gentleness arouse, thinking of their own sons and daughters and their own dreamy ambitions. By the time Neville left the public house it had begun to rain. He pulled up his jacket collar and pulled down his hat and wove through the wet streets towards the Childish Establishment. Thomas saw him from the window, across the road, and waved. Neville responded and stepped forward into the path of a heavy carriage. He was struck, said Thomas, directly in the chest, and slipped in the wet street, falling backwards so that he hit his head on the pavement as he fell crushed under the wheels. Thomas had rushed outside and run to the site of the accident. The carriage driver was distraught, and chattered incoherently with shock. Uncle

Neville was quiet. He lay with his face in the rain and his eyes tightly closed. He was already gone.

Thomas said: "I just sat in the rain, feeling empty, and unable to act. At last someone took my arm and guided me away. It was not like Dickens; it was base and awful and Neville looked disfigured and forlorn, the rainwater steaming with blood down his face . . ."

The skylight:

Something she loves: Lucy sleeps beneath a skylight. It is so like a photographic glass plate − a rectangle of dark possibilities within which features emerge. She wakes to see stars that have moved and the slight shifts of colour, and notices for the first time the many gradations of the dark. There is a purple stage and another where the sky has a slight coppery tinge. Then the space is reversed, becoming bone white in the mornings. In winter sometimes she woke to find a rectangle of snow held above her, a kind of magical *carte-de-visite*, with a message of frozen time.

One day, Lucy believes, one day in the future, people will discover how to photograph the vast night sky. They will sit behind a glass panel, and make visible these changes. They will show everyone the prodigious nature of the heavens, its positive/negative exposures, its blindings and enlightenings. Photographs of the night will convince everyone of the existence of God.

45

LUCY NOW FOUND HER OWN CULTURE A SHOCK. AFTER ALMOST EIGHT weeks in England, she was still thinking of India and feeling misplaced and dislocated. The radical modernity of London disturbed her – the clutter, the heavy clothes, the trams, the bells, the cash registers and the lampposts. English people seemed at once too large and too faint; they had pale faces and pale eyes and talked too much of the weather in their wet-wool clothes. The hops smell of public houses was sickening; Lucy could not pass by one without thinking mournfully of her dear Uncle Neville. These may be, she reflected, the forms that grief takes, this sense that everything is unmitigated and out of kilter. Standing on the corner of Oxford and Regent Streets she looked at the stream of people flowing by with their heads down and their coats pulled against the cold wind, and felt as they did: embattled, quashed, and by something as imprecise and irresistible as wind. Ellen was asleep in the wicker baby carriage Thomas and Violet had given her as a gift. She was too large now for its neat little newborn space. Occasionally someone peered in, and offered a compliment to the bonny baby, but more often Lucy and Ellen moved together as if in a bubble, invisibly asunder, enclosed in a depressed patch of air within the blustery currents around them.

Thomas had noticed his sister's low spirits and offered to seek out a tonic: he recommended Dr Whittles' – a pick-me-up, said Thomas, and highly effective. He also suggested attendance at his magic-lantern shows, so Lucy began to accompany Violet, sitting in a regular space reserved for her in the back row near the door, in case the baby became noisy. She had forgotten how odd and how exorbitant the images were – how deanimated and posed, rather like Victor Browne's photographs. They saw adventures, romances, shows on natural history. Each commenced with the rose-tinted slide of a fairy, holding up a flowery sign saying WELCOME TO ALL! One night they saw a show on the Indian Mutiny of 1857 and Lucy was dismayed at the India she saw enlarged and illuminated. A man in a British Army uniform stood at the front of the screen announcing the titles. He held up a curved sabre with each announcement.

"Savagery at Meerut!"

"Cowardly Sepoys defeated by English Bravery!"

"The Great Mutiny put down!"

"Our Soldiers Triumphant!"

"The Empire Retained!"

The last image was of the Viceroy, pompous, erect, beaming under a gold-coloured palanquin, topped by a star. The audience rose and applauded. In this vision Indians were a nation of snarling barbarians, with daggers in bared teeth and murderous attitudes, and the British a noble race, etched in classical style, uprighteous, valiant, bleached and pure. Lucy felt goose-flesh arise on her arms. She was chilled, upset.

"How ghastly," said Violet, when the lights came on.

Lucy remonstrated with Thomas after the screening, but he said it was a popular show and nourished the National Spirit.

"I am disgusted", Lucy said loudly, "by National Spirit."

Thomas and Violet exchanged glances; they both looked

surprised and critical. Lucy felt then the descent of an inner emptiness. Neville, she thought, would know what she meant. She experienced an acute sense of loneliness, a clouding of her self in the absence of understanding.

"Tomorrow", said Thomas, acting jolly, "we have *The Flying Dutchman!*"

"Which version?" Lucy demanded.

She made some feeble excuse or other, and with her baby carriage before her swept out into the street to cease the confrontation. It had been raining and the lamps had been lit and the city of London was transformed. There was a glossy black sheen cast over everything and solid buildings stood firm above their projected duplications; it was another kind of magic lantern, another visual effect which halted Lucy Strange in her steps. The creme stone of an otherwise ugly bank build-ing was remade as a quivery film of light. Gas lamps threw down diagonal lines of spots along the road. Huge edifices leaned into vacant mirrors. Lucy stood still in the cold, shiv-ering uncontrollably, wrapping her woollen shawl more and more tightly. She was bound to this contradiction: between the material and its ethereal incarnation in light. She had seen these reflections a thousand times: why did they rise up now with the force of revelation?

That night Lucy dreamed she met the dead author, Charles Dickens, walking in the street. He carried a lamp, like Diogenes, and his head was bent like a detective looking for clues.

"This way," Dickens kept saying. "Follow me. This way. I'll show you where it is."

He pointed with his beard, as Indians do, and had a gently persuasive manner and a comic appearance.

Ellen awoke Lucy before she discovered their destination or what they were seeking. Baby-cry rent the dream and pierced

186

the texture of the night. Lucy rose automatically, barely awake, and gathered in her daughter. She felt Ellen's hot convulsing body register her presence, slowly cease sobbing, and then, yet more slowly, begin to relax and settle. The sweet scent of breast milk. Her regular puffy breathing. Her sinking back, satisfied. Lucy fell asleep again immediately, the baby curved into her, a smaller true reflection of her own sleeping shape.

46

IN MID-WINTER IT WAS CONFIRMED: LUCY WAS ILL. THE DOCTOR harrumphed and made notes and fiddled absent-mindedly with his cufflinks and his oxblood tie. He had listened to her chest and found cavities where living lung should have been.

"Consumption," the doctor announced.

He looked over his eyeglasses with an air of strict professional gravity, but sounded, Lucy thought, oddly pleased with himself for the certainty and abruptness of his diagnosis.

In truth Lucy had guessed of her condition for some time. On the ship she had coughed a gob of blood into her handkerchief and seen — oh God — her own shining death. In an instinctive act she flung her sullied handkerchief overboard, and watched it fall into the foam wake, churn briefly and disappear. She had seen enough by now of street life in London and Bombay to know that blood-spitting was the greasy sure flag of mortality.

"Thank you," she said to the doctor, hearing the absurdity of her remark, wondering if doctors are accustomed to these inappropriate gestures of gratitude. He made a waving movement, a kind of dismissal, then commenced a cautionary lecture. She could return to normal relations with adults, he said, but must be aware of the special susceptibility of children. Distance, he said, tapping his pipe on the desk. Distance. She must drink a pennyworth of milk each day, and rest, and stay warm, and must not indulge in exertions of either the mind or the body.

Lucy watched the doctor's mouth move as he spoke; she judged him professionally dissociated, unconcerned. These things she instantly resolved: that Ellen must be protected from her breath; that Violet and Thomas should not be told, until it was no longer possible to conceal her condition; that she would resume, more seriously, her work of photography, securing whatever she was gifted or fated to see; that she would be brave, determinatively brave, and not consider, not for one moment, that a life abbreviated is a life diminished.

With the doctor's confirmation of her illness Lucy was distracted for a while, then resumed her usual life. Ellen made it easy. Babies pull attention in their direction; they require fuss, organisation and sensible decisions, new clothes and new amusements for their amazing enlargement. Lucy was practical, maternal. Lucy kept calm, kept her *distance*. But at night she was assailed by imaginings of her own inner body. She imagined her lungs like honeycomb, fretted into unsupportable organic sculptures, lacy with their own death-dealing dissolution. She imagined air moving through the corridors of her altered anatomy, not finding the route to fuel her breath, but leaking out in a slow, suffocating exhalation. She saw, above all, a kind of city, all caves and pipelines and underground tubes, rather like the ones engineers were now creating under the streets of London – the Metropolitan, they called it – a dark new geography. Once she had stumbled upon workers emerging from a gape in the street; they had skin made of earth and looked like a fraternity of the underworld. She saw them blink and look lost. They wiped their faces with rags. Bog men. Lazarus men. Creatures of sub-London dark.

Someday – this she knew – doctors would have an apparatus

to photograph the inner body. To light the dark. They would present patients with crimson images of their hearts and lungs; they would show the skeleton in all its fine ivory architecture; they would reveal the tunnelling waterways of the blood and the convolutions of the bowels. They would photograph the baby within the womb, swelling into being, furled in great expectation, waiting upon its own features in its mother's developing fluids. They would even, Lucy imagined, photograph the brain, and these photographs would have a lyric and lambent quality: they would be like pods of loveliness, like newly discovered planets, remote, elaborate, drifting on glass plates like secrets still unbroken.

47

LUCY HAD BECOME A WALKER. SOMETHING IN HER, SOME RESTLESSNESS
or sorrow or drive forward into life, compelled her to move
through this city as though she could claim its whole compass.
She strode out each day pushing Ellen — propped up now
because she could no longer lie with comfort in the confining
carriage — and walked from their new rooms in Stepney to
Stepney Green, then along Whitechapel Road to Houndsditch
Junction and down to the river along Bishopsgate. Sometimes
she crossed London Bridge and headed to Kennington Park,
one of her favourites. In another route she simply followed
without plan the sinuous curve of the Thames, crossing bridges
back and forth along the way. She knew all the bridge names
and landmarks, and carried in her head the shiny ribbon of
the Thames-shape she had seen on maps in the British Library,
its humps and bows and thinning out to the west, its bright
blue arterial representation that was nothing, nothing at all,
like its actual brown. Sometimes, if she had money, she took
the ferry to Westminster and then began walking west and
north, tracking the city through its parks: St James's, Green,
Hyde, up to Regent's, and then the long haul uphill to
Hampstead Heath. It was a secret mission: to gaze on the water-
shapes of rolling hills, to see again the world made extensive
and open.

Several times Lucy combined walking and a carriage ride to travel from Stepney to Kew Gardens. She stood in the glass and iron palm house and gazed at peepuls, pepper-vines, tree-plants and palms, remembering India. The pavillion looked like the product of whimsy or the emanation of a dream; its rainforest light, its population of tropical plants garnered from all points on the equator, existed in unnatural defiance of the nature around it. Lucy moved in from the cold, pushing at the heavy swing doors with the nose of the baby carriage, into the artificial warmth caught under the high glassy chamber, then she pushed out again, and felt the cold air sting her cheeks. This was allegorical knowledge: the world split into zones, the bodily registration of selves that were divided, multiplied.

Lucy had spent entire days walking in this way, returning after dark, looking hollow-eyed and exhausted, with blisters on her feet and a ragged ill look. Thomas thought privately that this walking was a mild form of madness, an incessancy, a refusal to rest, that his sister had carried over from her long ocean travels. He saw that Lucy had grown thin and bore hoops beneath her eyes that in some lights appeared like dreadful bruises. She looked woeful, he thought. She looked like a fallen woman.

It was only when Lucy began taking her camera with her on these journeys that she learned to pause, to see again and more carefully images taken and untaken. Thomas constructed a kind of wooden box at the end of the baby carriage within which she carried her photographic equipment. The camera stand lay like a pronged spear along the side of the carriage, bound against it with twine. The baby carriage now looked like a new invention, a contraption that transported infants as it caught the world on a three-pronged spear. Heads turned as Lucy passed; she might have been an inventor, an eccentric.

It was in the spring, on these walks, that Lucy met through the contemplative vision of her camera the two companions who would save her from death by loneliness. One day at Kew, she was bent beneath the dark cloth shroud of her camera when she saw through the lens a face that was unforgettable. Beyond the glass walls of the palm house rising up into the sunshine, she saw a woman strolling by herself with her eyes closed and her face tilted to the sky, as if absorbing as much morning warmth as possible. She wore a feathered bonnet and a copious gown with a brown checkered front panel. It was Mrs Minchin. The purple shape that so marked her was for Lucy the coloured shock of the past returned: she swivelled the camera on its stand and watched as Mrs Minchin, who seemed not to have changed or aged at all, slowly began walking in her direction, then halted ten feet away and stood still in an oval-shaped flowerbed of blue crocuses, as if waiting to be photographed.

Lucy could have remained hidden but instead called out.

Mrs Minchin opened her eyes and looked around rather blearily, as if her ears had deceived her.

"It's me," Lucy said loudly. "Lucy Strange. From Australia."

She heard her own voice ring out into the open spaces and gardens.

Mrs Minchin stared. Then she was at once upon Lucy, and embraced her like a long-lost prodigal daughter. Ellen began to cry and Lucy bent to lift her; at this act Mrs Minchin's eyes filled with tears and she reached forward and took the howling infant in her arms, soothing it at once with her low voice and the ample bed of her bosom.

"Now, now. Now, now."

"Let me look at you," Mrs Minchin said to Lucy. "So grown up. So like Honoria."

Then she added cannily: "Are you ill?"

Mrs Minchin had left Australia not long after Neville departed with the children. She stayed on until the house was sold, spending much of her time with blind Mrs O'Connor, but feeling bereft, distressed and alone in the world. Grief, she said, had almost destroyed her. It was like carrying a grey cloud over the heart. Like fog. Like blur. There were days when she cried for no reason, or sat staring at the wall, thinking in maddened ways of the children she didn't have. At length she found work as a nurse on a sea passage to England and had decided to stay, returning in London to her old profession of midwifery. Mrs Minchin now lived not far from Lucy – in Spitalfields – in a small room at the back of a building above a pharmaceutical store, from which leaked, she said, odiferous vapours. Lucy tried to imagine Mrs Minchin in her stinking room, resting on a narrow bed in her chequered dress, her purple face obscured, in a mote-filled light.

Now they were together in a place of incomparable greenness and unlikely coincidence. There were planted beds of daffodils, crocuses, tulips and pansies, and Mrs Minchin kept exclaiming at their prettiness then trampling them to pick samples for Ellen to chew at and tear. She was always leaving the paths and heading off to examine the Latin names pinned to the trunks of trees.

"*Prunus avium plena!*" she called out. She stood under a quivery cascade of full white blossom.

"*Hippocastanum!*"

"Horse Chestnut," called back Lucy. "I know that one."

All around the park decorous couples strolled arm-in-arm along the paths and entered and left the glass buildings with a sideways swish of a broad skirt, the collapse of a parasol, the removal of a hat. Mrs Minchin was unstoppable. She hitched up her dress and waded through flowerbeds and grasses, deviating from the paths to the sources of her own pleasure and attention. Lucy watched her form and saw within it a hefty liveliness. Her girlhood feelings of antipathy instantly evaporated. Here was a woman of spirit and gumption, cutting swathes with her body in order to shout out the name of a tree. She carried Ellen resting low and secure on her hip.

The photograph Lucy took of them had from the second of its existence the redolent quality of a remembrance of things past: it framed Mrs Minchin and Ellen under a canopy of *Prunus avium plena* blossom, looking like a grandmother and her beloved granddaughter. The tree formed a drooping soft dome-shape around them. Fallen petals lay on their shoulders and in the fine nets of their hair. Mrs Minchin's wine-stain face appeared as a face in deep shadow. The photograph seemed almost to convey the fragrance in the air.

All day the three cavorted together. Mrs Minchin had money: she bought a picnic of tea, scones and Spanish oranges, and later hired a smart pony-trap to carry them all home. They sat high watching London uncoil beside them. Ellen slept soundly in Mrs Minchin's arms; the stowed baby carriage and camera equipment rattled for the entire journey.

"We should live together," Mrs Minchin proposed.

"Yes, together."

"I mean it," said Mrs Minchin.

Lucy was drowsy. Her lungs tightened and ached as if they were being laced into a corset. She could feel an outbreak of cold sweat flooding at her forehead.

"Yes," she said softly, trying to sound neutral. She rested her head against the solid-fleshed woman beside her. Mrs Minchin. Rediscovered.

What accidental pattern of life delivers us our friends? What, our lovers? Might there be a plot within biographies arranged entirely by affections? It was at Hampstead Heath, barely two months later, that Lucy would meet her second companion. She was photographing one of the ponds, trying to reproduce with fidelity the sky and the trees reflected, tremulous as atoms, on the surface of the water. Ellen kept toddling in and out of the frame; she wore a lemon-yellow frock and a cheeky expression. There were strewn leaves, darting birds, and a breeze that kept troubling the quality of the reflection.

He must have been watching Lucy at work for some time. When she surfaced from the dark camera shroud, dreamily blinking, he stood beside her.

"Jacob Webb," the man said, proffering his visiting card.

He gave a small self-conscious bow, without taking his eyes from Lucy's face. He wore a fine cherry-coloured jacket and waistcoat over shabby trousers that were spattered all over with oil paint. Lucy noticed these first, before she looked closely at his features.

Jacob Webb was a tawny, tall man of thirty or so years. He had a large nose, straw hair and deep brown eyes. He was an artist, he said, living hereabouts, in Hampstead. He wished to employ her services as an artist's model. It was her face, in particular, that he wished to paint. Her face.

Lucy blushed at the directness of his speech and of his gaze.

"May I have the honour of knowing whom it is I am addressing?"

"Mrs Isaac Newton," Lucy responded. It was the first time she had ever called herself by this name.

"Ah, prisms!" the gentleman responded. "Whiteness shattered! The spectrum revealed!" He smiled as if he had just told Lucy a clever riddle. She must ask Isaac. Names were foolishly entailing.

48

Dear Isaac,

I write most of all to thank you for your words about Neville. To know that you remember him so fondly is a great comfort and consolation, and Thomas and I were moved by the loyalty and depth of feeling in your descriptions. Neville sounded both more comic and more serious than we knew him; perhaps, taking the parent role, he felt constrained with his charges and new responsibilities. In any case, Thomas has shown me the grave, which is a simple affair in a rather neat little churchyard, not far from where we live. My sweet sister-in-law, Violet, places flowers regularly upon it, although she knew Neville for less than one year.

My brother continues to thrive in his business. The owner of the Magic Lantern Establishment, a Mr Childe, has made him a partner, and together they entertain novel schemes and vast ambitions. Thomas is convinced, as I am, that there will one day be moving-picture shows, which tell stories not by posed scenes but by the simulation of life itself, in all its restless mobile spirit and colourful complication. Patrons will enter the lantern show as though they are entering a dream, and see before them apparitions in a kingdom of light. There will be new effects and new sensations — "partickler when he see the ghost!" — as Neville used to say; it will be a communing with spirits more brilliant than any seance could contact or conjure. Thomas and I talk often of this idea. Like some photographers in London he is using magnesium to create a *sudden flash of light, and though it is dangerous and volatile, believes something in its bright combustibility holds a key to the development of the magic lantern. Thomas is also experimenting with super-impositions and different lenses. He affixed a microscopic device to the magic-lantern camera and with the aid of a surgeon from the Royal College projected slides of cell life for training doctors to observe. I sat in the back row with Ellen and found the show a marvel — much more than the dreadful Mutiny I wrote to you about, or the endless, utterly conventional romances. Our inner substance, dear Isaac, is a series of blossom-looking cells, netted and sewn up with miniature veins and capillaries. We are plant life, it seems, and wonderfully intricate.*

The surgeon used a pointer to indicate areas of concern, but I could not follow his discourse, which was for doctors alone, and in a vocabulary largely incomprehensible. I found myself looking simply at the shapes before me, of which life itself — imagine! — is shrewdly composed. Thomas too was agog at this fleshly spectacle: when I saw him after the screening he was dumbstruck with awe and barely knew what to say. ("Partickler when he see the ghost.") Thomas does not believe, as I most assuredly do, that the living body may be one day photographed inside: for him dead cells are the peak of visual exploration. Nevertheless, he was deeply impressed and talked of nothing else for two weeks. I must add that Ellen writhed and was inattentive throughout the surgeon's show: how does one direct the vision of small children or assert which image is important or which inconsequential? Perhaps this can only be known by one's self. Perhaps we are not part of all we have met, but of all that we sensationally or passionately notice. What do you think, my dearest Isaac?

You ask for news of my work and I can report truthfully that my knowledge of chemistry is improving — largely through correspondence with the Society of Photographers — and that I am slowly mastering the wet collodion technique. Yes, I still stain my clothes and have a sprinkling of silver nitrate and powder stains on my hands, but am more careful now at mixing and decanting my collodion. As you know, the glass slide must still be wet with emulsion when the photograph is exposed, and for a long time I worried about the bubbles in the mixture and the appearance of thumbprints on the corners of the image. Now these seem to me charming, although the men of the Society of Photographers consider thumbprints a sin and me an irredeemable sinner for refusing their wise counsel and continuing wilfully to reproduce this faint mark of my own handiwork. The photograph should appear, one of them wrote to me, as if God had breathed it onto the glass. Reprobate that I am, I am still wedded to the maculate and the human sign, and accept now that my work will never be exhibited in the halls of South Kensington. If I could locate another woman interested in photography, I feel sure I could speak honestly and openly of these matters and defend more confidently my maculate aesthetic.

I too have been experimenting and wishing to find new effects. When I take the lens cap off to expose the plate, I count the seconds carefully, one to five, but have now been leaving the cap off longer, or shorter, and recording the results. I have been using albumen paper as well, and remember that in the factory we used to dry it as quickly as possible to achieve an extra sheen on the surface of the paper. There is some link between sheen and heat I have not yet discovered. I take care with my glass plates — much more than with the chemicals — and am keen to try emulsion on metal (they are called ferrotypes, or tintypes) which I believe have a dark mysterious look to them and would be more suitable for someone as accident-prone as myself. It is of course you, dear Isaac, who has made this unprofitable employment possible: I know you asked me not to thank you again for your payments, but — just one last time — I am grateful, more than I can say, for all the material assistance you have given me, and more than that for your encouragement in my faltering art.

My beloved Ellen remains the other true focus — there is no other word for it — of my time and devotion, and when she is able she too will utter thanks and embrace you as her honourable uncle. She has at last begun walking and launches herself into the world with a wild *toppling gait, jerky and wilful. She has no fear of anything, and charges towards water and birds and flights of stairs with truly alarming rapidity and sureness of intent. I have to keep sweeping her up in my arms to restrain this movement, and fear for her safety more often than not. She inhabits her body so robustly, and with such ease of spirit, and has an appetite for substances of many kinds. I caught her this morning with a mouthful of bright green leaves: she looked like some bloated insect creature, caught at herbivorous luncheon. I had to put my fingers deep into her mouth to extract all the leaves, and she screamed at me and wailed, as though I had robbed her of a boiled sweet. I delight in her presumption, her imperious claim to space, her loud, loud voice, her curly hair, the sight of her arms waving like a windmill as she runs off to each new and important adventure. At this stage Ellen seems largely uninterested in speech; Thomas says it is because she uses her mouth for everything else! (She calls him Tom-Tom, which amuses him greatly — he says she sees still within him his old Brazilian ambition — but she cannot manage "Violet" in any form or contraction.)*

Enclosed with this letter is my favourite photograph of Ellen. Although it is a little blurry, since she would not be bribed to stay wholly still (and the Society of Photographers, I must say, would berate me for displaying such an image) — you can see her quicksilver glance and her aspect of intelligence. The beguilement of infants resides not in their posed formality or settled good behaviour, but in these evasions of order, these clever rebellions. You must not think the image blunted, but on the verge of locomotion. And if you look carefully with your magnifying glass — as I did, seeking particular details — you can see a curved arc of light resting neatly in each eyeball which is the cheval mirror I set at the window to train more light into the room. This felicitous inclusion, this bent light that places my intention upon and within my daughter's face, excites and pleases me. It is another form of love, is it not, the studied representation? It is devotional. Physical. A kind of honouring attention. I think of photography — no doubt absurdly — as a kind of kiss.

Let me now tell you about my new friend, Mrs Molly Minchin. When I was a child in Australia the same Molly Minchin came to stay with us. She was a friend of my mother's, and a midwife, employed for the tragic birth I have spoken of to you. After the deaths of my parents she stayed on in our house, cooking meals, cleaning, trying hard to look after us. I despised Molly Minchin because in my grief-stricken reasoning I held her somehow responsible for my mother's death, and I also resented her presence and her act of substitution. Now I have re-met her — she was stomping about in Kew Gardens and reading Latin names with a clang as if she was ringing a brass bell. She has a sturdy vigour and openness to life which has quite revived me. I recognised her immediately because she carries a distinctive purple wine-mark, which covers one half of her face: this conspicuousness in the world has not marred or undermined her, but given her a resolute strength of character. I spied her through the lens of my camera and it was as if the long-past sprang phantomlike to confront me: I was afraid of a whiff of death, of some wound, or corruption, of something dark which would fly up like a bat and scratch at my face. I hid for a while, afraid, silently observing her in my black-out tent of velvet, before I saw her about to move on, and called out my own name.

Molly grew up in Madras, so we speak together of India. We also speak of Australia, and of her memories of my parents. I tried for so long to forget my parents, but think now that Molly's company is meant to return me to them. She has a fine collection of stories and a loving presence. Ellen adores her. We are both rescued from our loneliness, and I from the feeling of being perpetually foreign and from a country no-one else really knows of, or believes in.

It is late now and time for the gas lamps to be lit. I greet you, dear Isaac, from across the earth and the ocean. The sun will now be rising on Malabar Hill. Please send me any news of Bashanti, and the others. I miss the self that I achieved in my year in India. She was a little braver than I am and more wide-awake, more healthy, more receptive to what is new. This is, I suppose, why we pale fellows travel. To find

the person with these qualities, the one enfolded secretly, like a love
letter, in stuffy dank England or monumental Europe, or easy, remote,
complacent Australia.

I photograph you in my mind,
Your affectionate friend,
Lucy Strange

(By the way, what is the significance of your name?)

49

JACOB WEBB LEARNED AS A YOUNG BOY THAT NOTHING WAS FIXED BUT art. His father, a Nonconformist lay preacher and farmer in Nottinghamshire, taught him that the Bible was inerrant, that man was sinful, and that the hand of God was at work mysteriously in every accidental, or miserable, or minor catastrophe. God was always responsible, it seemed, for things that went wrong.

At the age of seven Jacob witnessed an astonishing hailstorm. It was deep mid-winter. The steely sky filled with stones the size of billiard balls, which catapulted with malevolent aim onto the heads of their chickens. Four died, knocked flat by the sky's sudden ice. Jacob's dog, Red, had been caught outside in the storm and cowered, whimpering softly, beside a rain barrel, so Jacob had to run like a madman through the hail to fetch him, and then half drag and half carry the poor animal towards the house. The air was crazy with missiles. He could hear the pounding of falling stones hitting the thatched roof, dropping into the hen-house, and bouncing off the woodshed; he could smell the pungent wet fur of his terrified dog; and he could feel the hard pellets of ice battering at his body. One caught his right shoulder with a sickening crack and another struck his outstretched arm. Foolishly, Jacob turned his face to the sky, and at that moment a hailstone hit him directly on the ear. He felt a pain like fire flash through the ball of his skull. He cupped his hand over his stinging and remarkably hot ear, and tugged hard at Red. But he was so confused and disabled that he was momentarily unsure in which direction they should move. The dog was lumpish and heavy and not helping at all. His own hands and feet were unendurably cold. Jacob thought: *I will die here, right here; this is a kind of punishment. And Red will die too, and so will more of the chickens, and there will be a huge grave to cover us — boy, dog and chickens — all lying mixed together.*

Jacob's father appeared from somewhere and gathered him in his arms. A great coat fell around the boy like the wings of an angel. It was a Miracle. Deliverance. These were words that he knew. His father ran directly to the house and lay him inside. Then he ran out again into the hail to rescue the dog. Jacob thought: *Praise the Lord, praise the strength of my father!*

Later he realised there was a thread of blood trickling from his ear, and that his mother was by his side, binding his head with a bandage. He seemed to swim in pain. Light was too intense. The room washed before him and then gradually settled. He could see his father smoking a pipe in the large chair beside the fireplace, and Red, apparently now at peace and sound asleep, resting his head gently on Father's feet. Jacob's sister, Ruth, who was older by ten years and moved in the world of adults, was calmly kneading dough at the table in the kitchen. Things looked the same, but were not. They would never again be the same.

When Jacob saw his body, the next morning, the top half was covered with bruises. "*Ring-streaked and spotted,*" it said in the Bible. The white bandage around his head looked like a little girl's Sunday bonnet. Jacob was ashamed to wear it. He hated the sight of himself. He felt that such a cataclysm in the sky, and his vision of the mixed grave, and the casually strewn corpses, all this was an augur of something awful to come. His slim blue body, there in the mirror, showed the direct violence of the hand of God. He was *"ring-streaked and spotted"*.

Jacob waited days for his presentiment of doom to be fulfilled, but nothing happened. Things were the same, after all. Then, two weeks later, just as he was beginning to relax and to doubt the sign of his bruised body, his father fell down in the meadow, gasping and gulping for air. His body was paralysed on one side and his mouth was fixed open. Tears flowed from his eyes, but his face was inexpressive. He lay prostrate, like an infant, his grey head resting where it fell, in mud and shit. Jacob stared down at his father and understood at once: this was it, worse than death, this prone, sad sight. Skin like meat, a marble eye, the stinking sully of sheep-mess and unmanly, mute immobility. Mr Nicholls, the cartwright who lived in the cottage on the hill, was summoned to help carry Jacob's father back to their house. Jacob stood stiff like a soldier and watched him slowly hauled up. His father's left arm was dangling like Christ's, in an old image he had seen of the deposition from the cross. His father half-dead, half-crucified. It frightened him to think about it.

At first everyone fussed and attended the patient with care. He could not move or speak, and was given to uncontrollable tears. Jacob saw how very aged his father suddenly looked, and realised for the first time that he was many years older than his mother. He knew nothing about how they met, or of their courtship, or of their mismatched marriage. Jacob read the Bible to his father and fed him porridge with a spoon. The slack mouth failed properly to take its nourishment. Jacob wiped his father's chin with a cloth and when he leaned very close he could smell death, sour death, lingering inside his open mouth. This was the man who had rescued him from the world of pelting ice. This was the man who had been as strong as an angel. Jacob wanted his father returned, his big strong father, not this ruin with a foul mouth and wet, wet eyes.

Jacob's father lived on for three more months, dying just days before his son's eighth birthday. He was laid out on the kitchen table, his arms folded to his chest like resting wings. Ruth and Mother hugged each other, and Jacob lay on the floor under the kitchen table, hugging his dog, Red. Grief was this stillness descending, this closing of bodies into the warmth of one another, this dull refraction of energy into few words and little movement. There was a smell of candle wax in the air and a chill mean draught. Heather scent and sheep stink flooded into the room. The fire had gone out. Jacob imagined sharp frost crystals suspended in the air.

The morning after the death Jacob did a remarkable thing: he crept to his father's bedside before anyone else had woken, and in the icy light of early morning, the light of brand-new death, carefully drew a picture of the corpse's face. With a lead pencil from the bureau he worked in the most calm and concentrated way that he could. It was quite a good likeness. It was clear and noble-looking. He kept the image all his life, convinced that it had within it a faintly Christlike aspect. Christ in an icy light. Christ in deposition. Christ gone cold.

50

SHE WONDERED WHAT DEATH WAS LIKE. WHAT ELLEN MIGHT SEE.

Fever had come upon Lucy and she had been sleeping and dreaming in the daytime, aware in her own body of the untimely derangement, conscious too of her irritation at being supine, and useless, and leaving Ellen in the care of Mrs Minchin. She realised she would begin to resent her illness, and that she would not, after all, be dignified and calm, but irascible, annoyed, a woman who fell into bed at eleven in the morning and woke three hours later still unrevived and vapid. Behind the veil of waking lay fragments of a dream about Rose, the woman from the albumen factory, beaten to death by her husband. Lucy had seen herself, once again, felled by his blow, and somehow in this dream she was both Rose and herself; somehow the taste of blood in her mouth was a fold back to the sudden irruption of violence and the blank shock of her fractured cheekbone and her cut swollen eye. Lucy could hear Mrs Minchin in the garden, talking to Ellen in the exclamatory tones adults offer to small children when showing them the world. Ellen made appreciative, high cooing sounds in response. Their voices were summery, normal. They sounded pure and joyful. She must rise, and make tea, and take Ellen into her arms. Her daughter was the instant cancellation of consumptive fever and bad dreams.

But Lucy lay in bed a little longer, turned her pillow to its cool side, and found herself dismissing the bloody dream to think about Jacob Webb. She had permitted him to call on her — to explain his work, he said — and he had arrived yesterday, at exactly ten in the morning, his head a smoky mass behind the frosted glass on the front door to the rooms she and Ellen now shared with Mrs Minchin. Lucy had paused a few seconds before opening, because Jacob Webb was their very first visitor, and she liked the round high shadow of his head, and the mystery of his features, effaced, patiently waiting. He looked like a grey flower, bobbing, set in a field of pearly light. She wondered whether it might be possible to photograph through blurry substances, whether a lens might be frosted, whether there might be filters or membranes or yet-to-be-invented substances that would produce effects like this, of a portrait undisclosed, of someone transformed to a floral effigy, just beyond human recognition.

When he was at last admitted Jacob Webb seemed inexplicably nervous. He wore once again his cherry-coloured waistcoat and jacket (with a pair of clean trousers, Lucy noted), but wasn't sure where to rest his hands and shuffled his feet as if he was on the verge of leaving. This evident self-consciousness surprised Lucy, since Jacob had seemed so bold and confident when they first met on the Heath. They shook hands and she bade him sit in their best armchair, while she perched on an upright one, her manner calm. Mrs Minchin had taken Ellen out for a walk, but first warned Lucy about strange men and their "designs".

"Probably a bohemian," was Mrs Minchin's parting sentence.

When Jacob was settled he looked around the sitting room and politely asked: "And your good husband? Mr Newton? Is he also at home?"

Lucy had looked at her ringless hands, then met Jacob's gaze.

"I have never been married," Lucy said outright. "I'm what righteous people call a fallen woman." She had decided to be honest.

Jacob was visibly taken aback. He blushed, averted his eyes and was silent for a moment. Lucy could hear Mrs Minchin's Swiss clock ticking on the mantelpiece. She thought with fondness of Max and Matilda Weller. Their supernumerous timepieces, all tyrannically stilled.

"Who is to say", Jacob replied at last, "who among us is fallen? And who – only God decides – is truly righteous? Forgive me; I had not meant to pry."

Lucy watched as the young man was recessed into his own thoughts; she imagined him in the act of falling backwards into a woven text of childhood homilies and churchy injunctions. *A fallen man.* Perhaps he was repelled, his response a type of embarrassed good manners.

"So there is no Isaac Newton?" Jacob persisted, sounding absurd.

"My benefactor," Lucy rejoined. "The patron of my photography."

"Ah. Just so."

A stalemate, Lucy thought. He wants an excuse to leave. She heard again the infuriating tick-tock and understood Mrs Weller's sensible objection. And then he surprised her.

"May I have the honour", he carefully asked, "of viewing some of your photographical images? If it is not presumptuous. If it is not inconvenient."

He looked at her directly.

"Since, after all, we are both artists," he added kindly.

So it was that they met in this way station of exceptional candour and found themselves standing, side by side, peering at Lucy's art. Jacob put his face very close to the image, then moved back, then forward again, squinting slightly, as if it were an oil painting he was viewing, and not the flat uniform surface of a photograph.

"Very fine," he murmured. He was looking at a blotchy heathscape, riddled with shadow.

"And this too. Very fine." (A carbon-print portrait of Ellen asleep.)

Lucy was aware of the proximity of Jacob's body. The brush of his elbow. His slim jutting hip. Seduction, she thought, is never face to face; it is this side-by-side permission of inadvertent currents and connections. This galvanism of bodies alerted to each other. This prickling charge.

Lying in bed, with Mrs Minchin's and Ellen's voices still playing in the garden, hanging there like a kind of human music, Lucy wondered what contract they had entered into. This man also knew the consoling intimacy of images and the ardour that attaches to representation. Jacob Webb was polite to the point of impersonality, yet she glimpsed in him – as indeed he may have glimpsed in her – inalienable conviction and lunatic love. She liked his fidgety hands and his abashed courtesy. The large feet shuffling in restless agitation. Most of all she liked his response to her work: he had paused, captivated. He had the remote look of someone hauled into a state of hallucination. And when he returned to her presence he spoke in soft enquiring tones, like a foreign traveller unsure, asking careful directions. After they parted, she found she missed him. Something in his tentative manner, his interiorised concentration, seemed to Lucy a familiar and comfortable thing, an unqualifiable intimation or presumption of affinity.

She wondered again what death was like. Was it the eradication, above all, of these selves brought into being in such small unspeakable moments, the self swaying between consciousnesses. Was it a halting of the sway? A negating rest?

Lucy turned in her bed. Perhaps something more simple: one wrestled with an angel and found oneself winning.

51

SHE WAS ON HAMPSTEAD HEATH, RESTING, HER EYES GENTLY CLOSED against incipiently stormy weather. Something redolent in the thrashing trees in the wind — their fierce breathy noise, their implication of wavy currents — made Lucy think again of the sea voyage that had returned her to England.

It was on this journey she had realised her life was a tripod. Australia, England and India all held her — upheld her — on a platform of vision, seeking her own focus. These were the zones of her eye, the conditions of her salutary estrangement. On the ship Lucy had befriended a sailor, Jock. He was a dour man of sixty or so, who shared her fascination for the ocean and its curious light effects. He joined her on the deck in his small leisured moments to talk in hushed confidences of his nautical passions. Lucy told him of the systems of exposure in photography that might capture sea-pattern or cloud, and of the chemical immersion that fixes the sheen of light upon water. Everything that is seen, Lucy told him, will one day somewhere be registered. No matter how fleeting. How slight. How apparently ineluctable. Jock the sailor was unconvinced. He would show her, he claimed, something which could not be trapped. For ten days Lucy and Jock watched the sunset together. On the eleventh day it happened: *the green ray*. There is in the mystery of receding light a casual, curious moment in which, by some rare combination of refraction and the angle of descending beams, the sun itself flashes green for three or four seconds, just before it tips half the world into darkness. Lucy definitely saw it. It was unmistakable. Sailors everywhere across the globe call this phenomenon the green ray. The sky was ribbed with light. The sky resembled, Lucy thought, a silken sari enfolded, its colours flashing just as the moving body animated the ridges and valleys of a garment.

In London Lucy opened her eyes to emerald green and a sea of white cumulus. It was summer now, and the air was windy and warm. She could see Ellen by the pond and Mrs Minchin bending over her. Ellen's bonnet had blown backwards and jiggled at her neck, and Mrs Minchin held her own hat with one hand and with the other was reaching for the child. Their dresses heaved and slapped in the unstable air. A ribbon flew out and fell back: all was adjusting; all was transient.

Mrs Minchin will be a mother, after all.

Lucy was consoled and unconsoled. They looked beautiful together. They possessed a truly rare and solar refulgence.

52

JACOB WEBB WAS SWEATING WHEN LUCY OPENED THE DOOR. HE appeared flushed and over-heated and removed his hat inelegantly, as a kind of afterthought.

"Good day," Jacob said, bowing slightly. "I have come to take you, if I may, for sweetened ices."

Mrs Minchin, who was standing behind Lucy, was warming to Jacob.

"Jolly excellent idea," she loudly announced. "Ever a pleasure to partake of a gentleman's ices!"

Lucy smiled. This man before her with rosy cheeks and a shy disposition had visited unannounced three times in the past week, and at each occasion the household – Molly, Ellen and she – had greeted him more happily. Ellen came stumbling forward and Jacob swept her into his arms, whereupon she sloppily kissed him. He was a man at ease with children but uncomfortable with women.

"Ices?" he repeated, to hurry them along.

The party of four – appearing to all the world like a family – sat together at wooden benches talking of the heat and of India and of the difficulties of being foreign. Jacob Webb expressed a fervent wish also to be foreign, to be *strange*, he said. He liked, he insisted, the way Lucy and Mrs Minchin saw things more keenly and with resources of comparison and exotic assessment. He wanted his too-English vision transformed. He wanted to see things, he added, as Lucy did, intact and evident in their stunning visibility. Lucy was flattered, pleased. She was about to respond when Ellen, who had been wriggling on her lap, leaned forward across the table and upset a glass of raspberry cordial, so that it splashed and discoloured her. Ellen let out a howl and waved her chubby arms, and every customer in Stevenson's Palace of Confections turned judgmentally to comment and look. Without hesitation, Jacob took out a handkerchief and began dabbing Ellen clean. He held her chin with his thumb and forefinger — as Lucy recalled her own father doing — as he wiped her wet face. This was the moment, the very moment, that Lucy Strange fell in love with Jacob Webb. He was tenderly intent on cleaning Ellen, who wore the puzzled sodden look of children recovering from alarm. Jacob was leaning very close, slanted to his task, and at some point he raised his gaze to Lucy's face.

"A mess," he said, blushing.

Lucy leaned slowly forward, took his finely bearded chin between her thumb and forefinger, and kissed Jacob Webb very softly on the mouth. She could feel Ellen snuggling against her, trying to reclaim attention, and the force of Mrs Minchin's approving stare. It was a wholly perspicuous and perfect act. Jacob smiled widely. Love was this sudden clarification, this rightness of gestures and feelings. This sweet solemnity. All my images, thought Lucy, all my noticed oddities and recorded visions, recruit to this simple event, here, eating ices on a summer's day, in London, England, in 1871. She was nineteen years old and had knowledge enough to understand the veracity of her own responses and intelligence enough to be troubled by their hazardous implications. For Jacob, too, this was a moment of confirmation. He thought: I will marry this woman, I will adopt her child, I will speak to her of all I sincerely guard, of my family, of my worries, of my peculiar childhood, and most secretly of all, of my yearning to create an artwork that summons one, just one, sure and precise memory, immediate as a photograph — *my father standing in the doorway, knocking snow from his boots, his warm breath visible as a blurry feather. He unwraps from his neck a long blue scarf and holds it at arm's length, as though it is the serpent that tempted Eve. Behind his head snowflakes churn in the whitish air and his face is bright, alive.*

After the occasion of the ices and the spilled raspberry cordial, Lucy and Jacob contrived courtship outings in the evening, so that they could speak and act more freely. Together they visited Thomas at the Childish Establishment and Jacob saw there images he considered intoxicatingly profane. Oriental dancers with naked midriffs. Scenes of luscious cruelty and fantastic barbarism. Monstrosities. Titillations. He did not speak of this to Lucy, but wondered at her maturity and her intimidating worldliness. In the pavilion of wild images she was entirely at home. She accepted everything with curiosity and sincere equipoise. Her brother Thomas was a good-hearted and matter-of-fact fellow, and his wife Violet, Jacob thought, somewhat shallow and silly, but of one thing he was certain: there was no-one else in the world like Miss Lucy Strange; she was a woman of singular and remarkable intensity. She was also a woman with an exquisite collar bone, deep sensuous eyes and an allure he could barely bring himself to name.

For Lucy, being liberated into the night was a gift. Apart from amorous possibilities (of which she dreamed and speculated), she loved the sublime spell of gas-lit London. Along the streets were rhyming pools of light and shadow, since gas lamps seemed to have a very definite compass, and extended only in limited, interspersed circles. She loved moving in and out of these spots of lights, watching the uneven flaring and waning, and listening to the whistle and buzzing sounds that ran mysteriously through the pipes. She loved too the retail stores that manufactured splendour: Moses and Son, the tailors, had massive metal chandeliers, all arabesque and curlicue, which flared prodigiously, and the butchers in Drury Lane unscrewed the burners of their gas pipes, so that light came streaming and fluttering, with lurid effect, above their displays of now unnaturally glossy meat. Women in wing-shaped dresses swept like moths between the lights, and men in top hats looked decapitated, blotted by darkness, as they moved at certain angles of casting shadow. It was a city transformed, shiny; the night itself was converted.

All this brilliance made Lucy delirious with pleasure. She took Jacob's hand and dragged him through streets, now nothing less than a gallery of spectacles. Gas-London was, she believed, its true form and character: it was artificially lovely and splendid to behold. When she peered into the future she knew that London would for ever be illuminated by gas; no other industrial technology would exceed or supplant it. In the future gas lamps would be consummate works of art, and every city, in every country, would honour its wavering flare.

Jacob considered Lucy's attraction to ignited spectacle incomprehensible. He had heard of "mooners", people whose superficial pleasure it was to roam the streets at night, glancing into shop windows and skipping between lit spaces, but Lucy seemed more serious than that, and more bent on aesthetic extrapolations. She introduced him to the Cremorne Pleasure Gardens, a dance platform with music and wine and multitudinous gas lights, a place of lewd movement and women giggling with their heads thrown backwards, glasses spilling ale, cigar smoke and jocularity, and he struggled to see what enchantment resided there. (Lucy had leaned close and whispered straight into his ear: don't worry, my love, I shall teach you to dance – as if she had read and divined his innermost fears.)

Walking home, one evening, Lucy halted and pointed, her arm extending. On one side of the street, the gas lamps were serially ranged; on the other, was a collection of gig carriages, waiting outside the Princess Theatre for closing, their gig lamps spaced perfectly and uniformly lined.

"In the future," pronounced Lucy, "people will understand that life is not a series of gig lamps or gas lamps symmetrically arranged; it is more encompassing, more immersing, more like an ulterior halo. Life", she continued, sounding oracular, "is a kind of semi-transparent envelope, in which we see, in which we feel, in which we fall in love. One day someone will write this," she added confidently, "and it will be understood as a proclamation."

Jacob was aghast. The woman he loved, the *strange* woman, spoke in stagy speeches and entertained supernatural visions. She spoke like someone who was watching history unfold, like someone who knew beforehand of her own death, and was speaking posthumously. He suddenly recalled a tale from school. Ulysses wants to consult with the prophet Tiresias, long dead, so he must visit the entrance to Hades to summon him forth. After pouring libations of many kinds to entice the dead to return, he finally sacrifices one black and one white sheep, and then the bloodless dead sweep forward, thirsting for the liquid of life. What Ulysses had not foreseen was the appearance of his mother, Anticlea. She had died of grief during his long absence. Ulysses must fight off his own mother, and all the other shades, to keep the precious blood solely for Tiresias. It distressed Jacob to remember this obscure tale now. Unbidden, he had glimpsed Lucy in another realm. In this context of so many night-lights and revelations, he had perhaps glimpsed her own certainty of her coming death.

Lucy watched her lover Jacob Webb meditating in a shadow. She reached forward and took his hand, pulling him into a pool of light.

"You're too grave," she said, touching a single finger to his moist open mouth.

"Let me enlighten you."

She would take this young man into her body. She would teach him all the forms of bioluminescence. She wanted to say this, to invite him in, but felt shy, wordless. Instead, she saw in a moment-not-yet-arrived his head dip in a tender arc, cautiously, lovingly, and offer her left breast an encompassing kiss.

53

HER *SPECIAL THINGS SEEN* AND *PHOTOGRAPHS NOT TAKEN* BEGAN TO flash at her, disarrayed. Time was feverish. Was this, Lucy wondered, an effect of her illness? Would death be a sudden accession of vision from all the times and images she had known? It was not morbid curiosity that stopped her in the street to look up at the sky and wonder aloud such things. She looked into clouds and had a spacious, empty-headed feeling. Heaven was already entering her. She was already becoming pure space, a chamber of images.

Bashanti and her mother:
This image returns and returns: Bashanti leaning her amber cheek against her mother's black hair.
A strange woman appeared in the kitchen and was preparing food. Lucy entered to fill a jug with water, and there she was, a small figure in a white sari, behaving as if the house was her own. "Good morning," said Lucy. But the woman said nothing: she bent her head, a minute inclination to acknowledge the memsahib's presence, but otherwise seemed barely to glance away from her task. She was frying onions and spices for the preparation of dahl; chilli, cumin and mustard-seed fragrance fizzed in the air. Lucy passed with her jug, staring at the

old woman, but realised she was being deliberately ignored.

Bashanti's mother – Isaac did not know her name – had been told many times to stay away, but came uninvited to the house to help Bashanti, to steal food (so Isaac said) and to sit in the sun with her daughter, whispering secrets.

For the first time Lucy realised that her servant was probably her age; her mother was youthful, perhaps forty, and seen together they were unmistakably mother and daughter: their faces were definite but imprecise mirrors – the same high foreheads and serious eyes, the same full mouths and pointy chins. Bashanti was taller than her mother and when they spoke she bent her head as if wanting to equalise their stature.

After her work in the kitchen Bashanti's mother went outside to sit on the back steps. She was threading flowers for *prasad*, for her holy duties. A pile of marigolds lay to her left and she was linking them in a chain that grew like a golden snake before her. Bashanti approached her mother from behind, knelt at her back, and then placed her face softly against her mother's hair. A curved brass bowl on a field of jet black. It was a gesture so simple and tender Lucy felt a sob and constriction in her throat and the revenant claim of something far, far away. She wanted to tell Bashanti of her private thoughts and memories and to chisel open the silence each was accustomed to. But it would have been such an impertinence to speak. There they were, very still, Bashanti appearing like a statue of devotion, her mother the quiet solid plinth of support, resting in a moment that was theirs alone.

Lucy understood then why Bashanti, who knew English, refused to speak it: to keep her own world intact. To keep it safe.

The night ascent:

Just before Lucy left for India, so long ago now, she had been abroad at night, in a parting outing, with Thomas and Neville. They had walked together for the first time to the Cremorne Pleasure Gardens and seen there a balloon lifting up into the sky. It was a gigantic inflation, a black-and-white striped pumpkin, rotund, ludicrous, sailing fantastically upwards. Passengers hailed down excitedly as they floated away. Uncle Neville agreed they should try it — when it's daylight, he said — but Lucy begged and implored for a night ascent. Neville at last conceded: how could he refuse his niece — soon bound for Bombay, for Isaac — any parting gift? In the end Thomas and Lucy rode upwards together; they waved to Neville as he stood below, a glass of ale in his hand, smiling happily.

The logic of forces that drives a balloon is bewildering and magical. Lucy felt the shudder of the cloth ball, straining above them, and the waywardness and contingency of their route into the sky. Noise fell away, breeze uprose, and there was only the roar, now and then, of the balloon's inspiration. When they bent to peer over the edge they saw London enflamed; the physical geography of the city had been remade by gas light, so that the main streets were rivers of light and the Thames a pitch-dark canyon, and the shopping districts were redrawn in legends of gold. "A fire map" was what the ballonist called it, and Lucy was delighted to think of London in this way: the Great Fire of London — not an abolition or destruction, but a miracle of gas. Elevation was joy: she must remember this. Overhead, the crescent moon was a meek contestant.

When they descended Thomas and Lucy were like

bubbling children. They chattered and leapt about. They embraced each other heartily. It had been, Lucy said to Neville, a true "sensation" And only later, falling asleep, hearing Neville's regular snoring close by in the next room, did Lucy remember the story of the Flying Dutchman, and thought then fleetingly, only fleetingly, of her mother, and her father, and of all the old sadness, and of distant Australia, and of all that was now everlastingly gone.

The geranium:

An image from long ago. How old was she, then? There is Mrs O'Connor, feeling her way around the back door with her claw-like left hand. In her right she carries a teapot without a lid. Mrs O'Connor raises the teapot and flings an arc of old tea leaves over a scrawny coral geranium, which nestles, somewhat neglected, just behind the back step. The plant is spattered with tea. Mrs O'Connor feels for the remains, which she scoops with her fingertips, and these too she flicks upon the besmirched geranium. Lucy watches her silently. She admires the confidence of the woman who lives in the dark. This woman who mucks the world so casually and with no meanness and ill feeling, leaving it speckled behind her.

The holy man:

Lucy had come upon a man naked, but for a smear of grey ash. His hair was matted and his body pitifully thin, and he bore on his forehead three white clay stripes: a Naga sadhu, Isaac explained. Isaac had been suspicious of what he called Lucy's attachment to Indian extremities; he thought she succumbed far too easily to beggars and charlatans, and was too impressed by ragged prophets and skeletal children, by wailing paupers and sneaky fakirs. But she had set up her cumbersome camera apparatus, manipulated wet glass, hid beneath her sheath, and photographically reproduced him. To Isaac this was indecorous, a form of obscenity. To Lucy, looking now, in over-dressed England, at this man who willed his own deprivation so as to achieve holiness, it was a form of honour. The naked ash-smeared man, vague as a spectre, appeared to her beautiful. He looked proud, assertive. He looked worthy of his image. The stripes on his forehead looked like head-lamps to guide his way.

The hat:

One day, she thought, there will be a device for capturing the likeness of something that happens very rapidly, or even instantaneously. Lucy had seen a marvellous sight that she wished it possible to record. Strolling with Mrs Minchin, holding Ellen on her hip, they had one night seen a gentleman's hat catch fire. He had been walking past one of the butcher's undisciplined gas lamps, when a spurt of flame shot out, a great hungry tongue, and caught his top hat. It must have been coated with some excessively flammable substance, for it instantly lit and spread over the surface, creating a hat-shaped flame at the poor man's head. He screamed and ran about, panicked and insensible, not having the wherewithal to remove the hat, until someone caught him, tackled him, and knocked it from his head. Ellen's eyes were excited and blazing with what she had seen; Mrs Minchin tut-tutted the butcher's irresponsibility, and Lucy saw in the event a new kind of art: the accidental application of wondrous anomaly. Imagine, she said, a painting of a burning stone. A burning bed. Even a burning giraffe.

54

LUCY HAD SPENT MANY YEARS CONTROLLING THOUGHTS OF HER mother's death, and Violet returned them to her with turbulent power. Within what seemed just a few months of their marriage, Violet was decisively and joyously pregnant, and Thomas full of the wry, baffled pleasure of fathers-to-be. Lucy was overjoyed at the prospect of a new baby in the family. She would advise and help Violet, and their children would love each other. Mrs Minchin would assist and they would all reconfigure their love in the endlessly elastic shapes that children create and inspire. But it was clear almost from the beginning that something was wrong. Violet found spots of blood staining her undergarments and felt frightening, obscure, stomach-clenching pains. Mrs Minchin advised as much bed rest as possible, so Violet gave up her piano teaching – leaving behind a whole class of disappointed girls – to concentrate on the careful nurturance of her child. Thomas fretted and became clumsy to the point of clownish collisions, and Max and Matilda Weller, alike in their concern, entrenched themselves as fixtures in the crowded house. Thomas found their presence an additional strain: they were fussy eaters and had lifetime habits of bizarre particularity. They wanted their tea the correct tone of pink, baths with specially purchased salts, and readings from the Bible at nine the morning and again at nine at night. Mr Weller brought some of his disembowelled clocks with him to the house and they lay dangerously strewn, a sorrowful disassembly.

When the catastrophe came, it was a gory miscarriage, sparing the life of the mother but ruining for ever Thomas and Violet's plans and leaving them wrecked and sobbing, lying together on a bed still damp with blood. Lucy found them clutching at each other like orphan siblings in a fairy tale. Mrs Minchin gave Violet a laudanum draught to help her sleep, and later that evening Lucy saw her cradling Thomas, holding him across her lap in a large velvet armchair. He had his head resting at her bosom and was crying softly. Mrs Minchin stroked his hair and whispered motherly condolences.

"Now, now," Lucy heard. "Now, now. Now, now."

It was like a screen suddenly perforated, with darkness leaking in. Lucy had largely left her parents behind, veiled by journeys, new countries, lovers, Ellen, but now found reminiscences and bad dreams returning to disturb her. There is some point in life at which one begins fully to imagine one's parents. Story fragments and memories begin to coalesce with force, begin to claim recognition and settle into human specificity. No longer figureheaded cut-outs or icons of power, they resolve into individual adult shapes, compellingly intimate. Lucy moved beyond the blue chrysanthemum fan, that fixed her mother at the point of enclosure and removal, to remember her inordinate fondness for the novel *Jane Eyre*, the objects in her wardrobe that spoke of idiosyncratic affections, the ribbon – why that? – uncurled to reveal "I adore you". She remembered too a whole repertoire of gestures and sayings, even small moments of unremarkable contact, described by a hand reaching forward, the brushing of hair, or the sweep of a dishcloth over a grainy table. Then she moved on, travelling perhaps on the silken road of the ribbon, to imagine her mother, Honoria, with her own autonomy, with suitors and love affairs, her mother kissing a stranger, her mother touching her own breasts, her mother frustrated or lonely or with unfulfilled ambitions. Her mother, further still, wracked by loss and haunted by absences, which were so private she could not even whisper them in the dark, to her husband, asleep, lying quietly beside her. Then Lucy at last recalled the day of Honoria's death, her glimpse, through the narrow cleft of a doorway, of her mother straining on the bed, rising up, screaming, her high belly sweat-glazed and shockingly naked. Mrs Minchin's large body moving to close the door. The footfall afterwards. The sight of Mrs Minchin, bloody to the elbows, washing herself off in a white enamel basin. Then her father, distraught. His face smudged by fatigue. His brown-and-white striped pyjamas. His disappearance. Lucy at last allowed herself to grieve. She locked herself in her room, claiming a return of fever, and wept, at intervals, uncontrollably. She wept for her mother and for her remote gentle father. She remarried them in their tragedy and put them together to rest. When Lucy recovered her composure, she felt herself finally an adult. She re-entered the world – pulling down the bodice of her gown, tidying her hair – to offer Thomas and Violet her strength, to nurture her inimitably beautiful daughter, and to make love to the shy artist, Jacob Webb.

Violet sat in a wicker chair, a woollen rug across her knees, as Lucy read aloud to her from the sentimental novel, *Jane Eyre*. Ellen played on the floor like a kitten, with balls of coloured wool, and Mrs Minchin sat very still, sombrely knitting. They were their own community. At length Mrs Minchin rose to make tea, and to cut for each of them a slice of marble cake, and they sat together over their repast, eating slowly and talking in hushed friendly tones. Ellen decided to crumble her cake in her fist, and Mrs Minchin tut-tutted with a counter-manding smile. Violet spoke of her love for Thomas and her fear that she had disappointed him, and Mrs Minchin and Lucy both lovingly consoled. Lucy explained that one might consider love analogous to the development process of photography: there are careful ministrations, the application of cautious shifts of shadow and tone, vision, patience, an oblique shimmering process, then the final achievement of something definite and recognisable.

Violet paused to consider.

"Not really," she said.

"No," Lucy agreed, with a conceding smile. "Not really. In fact, not at all."

They exchanged sweet glances; they loved each other.

Mrs Minchin rose to draw the curtains and let afternoon light into the room. A beam of turmeric yellow fell like a wand across the floor. The effect provoked in Lucy's heart a sense of jubilation.

"*Camera lucida!*" Lucy exclaimed, making a joke. But neither Violet nor Mrs Minchin understood.

55

IT WAS WITH THE MOST PASSIONATE CONCENTRATION THAT JACOB sketched her. He settled Lucy before him, posed on a chaise longue, her head tilted slightly away, her hands folded in her lap, and set about rendering her countenance in a way that would display, he hoped, her own artistry, inwardness and definition. She had a broad face, blue eyes and dark curly hair, but was not typically attractive or conventionally fair; rather she was, above all, distinctive. Jacob shaded and cross-hatched and recorrected outlines; he entered his labour as one enters a tunnel, with acute directed vision for the illuminated spot up ahead. Then he surprised himself by being rather pleased with his efforts — the first sketches were fulsome and honourably true. He was reminded of the time, as a boy, when he sketched the face of his dead father: it had been a similar act of untypical clarity — the force of circumstance, orbiting around death itself, had given his hand preternatural skill, just as now, in adoration, he knows the shape of his beloved. In truth, he is a little afraid of Lucy Strange. She is more intelligent than he, more bold and more brave. And photography has without doubt made her a seer; she is a woman of the future, someone leaning into time, beyond others, precarious, unafraid to fall.

"Behold me," Lucy silently entreated.

Lucy watched Jacob Webb sketch her in preparation for a painting. His reserve had fallen away; he stared at her with a piercing directness. At the same time, he was locked into his own task, radically alone, as artists are; he was self-communing and somewhat opaque. Around the room lay a dozen portraits at various stages of completion: Jacob specialised in a kind of prettified counterfeit, depictions of ladies in ruffled hats, children in neck bows, gentlemen with barrel chests and watch chains and solid leaden postures. Each figure was, she was sure, a reasonable likeness, but there was also a pastelly unfocused quality to the paint that made everyone appear more decorative than human. There was a gentleness, too, which Lucy recognised.

When she rose, for a break, to look at the sketches, Lucy was delighted to see that Jacob had included the silver-nitrate stains on her hands.

"Certainly my most maculate feature," she told him.

Jacob smiled, but had no idea what she meant. Then Lucy slid her spotted hand into a gap in Jacob's shirt, felt the skin on his chest, and drew him to her. She began unbuttoning his shirt, but he stepped back, a little alarmed.

"Permit me," Lucy said quietly. "Permit me to show you what I feel."

Lucy undressed Jacob Webb with delicate and deliberate slowness, learning his beauty inch by inch, feeling her own arousal at the aureoles of his nipples, the concave near his hips, the tufts of hair, the pink swelling penis. She led him naked to his bed, placed him there, then began, equally slowly, undressing herself, removing garments with taut and erotic delay, watching him watching her, enjoying his gaze. When she was undressed she lay her full body over his, then slid down, with delicious friction, to take him into her mouth. As he began to breathe more heavily, she raised herself over him and made love from above, watching his face. Jacob had a look of incredulity. Filamented lights shone in his eyes. Lucy moved her hips, helping him, creating their rhythm, and when at last he fell upwards, into her warm body, she collapsed downwards into him, her face hot and reddened, her own pleasure complete. Jacob had tears streaking his cheeks. Lucy lay there on his body, feeling him still inside her, their faces intimately together. Jacob's arms were around her: he held her tenderly.

After a long silence Jacob said: "Thank you."

Then, after another silence, and in a tone of apology, he added: "I'm sorry, Lucy. I have no words."

Quietness descending. Bodies coming down slow. Their little room an everywhere.

"Bioluminescence," Lucy at last responded, kissing him again.

56

LOOKING AT PHOTOGRAPHS CRACKED OPEN TIME.

Lucy Strange saw both the past and the future. She saw faces already changed, persisting eternally young, and the faces of the dead, docilely revenant. She saw lucent intimations of worlds to come. She saw unmade forms and inchoate presences. Images had trans-historical power. In the future, Lucy imagined, glass photographic plates would be serialised like the slides at Thomas's magic-lantern show, to fabricate a private machine for seeing. These would exist in homes, not in theatres, and families would crowd around them after dinner and watch as the space of glass transmitted visions of great beauty. The screen would glitter like mercury, and like mercury, ever shift. There would be a new form of community, riveted to vision. Lucy saw in the future a multiplication of the weird Medusa power she had seen many times in the Childish Establishment: people captured, eyes shining, by remarkable light, people lassooed willingly into vitreous fictions, people gambling on the wealth of a silver screen. Just as she saw Chinamen and Turkish dancers and the Niagara Falls, people in the future would see in their glass boxes improbable conjunctions and fabulous spectacles and the play of a million astounding images. They would find solace in the incontestable evidence of anything photographed. Anything at all.

57

HER FEVERISH ILLNESS MADE LUCY SUSCEPTIBLE TO IN-BETWEEN STATES.
She woke from a dream in which she had been performing
the entire photographic process – handling the syrupy, sticky,
collodion glass plates, sensitising them in a solution of silver
nitrate and potassium oxide, placing the plate in the camera
holder while it was still wet, exposing the plate, then
developing it in a solution of pyrogallic and acetic acids. In the
darkroom she removed the negative from the developer,
washed it in water, fixed it with a solution of sodium thio-
sulphate to remove excess silver oxide, washed it once again,
and finally set it to dry. This entire act – together with all the
correct chemical labels and proper sequence of actions – had
been performed disincarnate, as though she were a kind of
spirit, doomed to filmy repetition of what she knew best. Lucy
decided she must take a final series of photographs, one that
would constitute her valediction forbidding mourning. She
would allow error and chance – ripples in the collodion, over-
and under-exposures, bright whitish patches or unexpected
shadows – to enter her work, welcomed, as a mark of
relinquishment of control.

Lucy took a series of portrait photographs, wishing to record
each person she loved. There was a particularly lustrous image
of Jacob Webb; he seemed to emit light, as those in love

sometimes do, and certainly he appeared in the photographs more handsome than usual. He had a glint in his eye and an expression of sensual compliance. Lucy added a blind stamp – her initials embossed in the corner of the photograph. It was perhaps an unforgivable mark of possession, but she had been finally unable to resist. In the future, she would like Jacob to look at his own image, and to see in the corner, faintly, her timeless salutation.

Lucy also took many photographs of Ellen. These were less successful, since she so hated sitting still, but there were one or two, in particular, that showed all her restrained energy and fullness of life. In one photograph, Ellen was showered with lamplight, giving her frizzy hair a gorgeous divine glow; in another she looked unusually thoughtful and child-serious, with an endearing pout and self-possession. In a third photograph Ellen was holding a bunch of lilacs. This was a concession to Mrs Minchin, who wanted something pretty, she said, something more like the studio portraits she had seen in shop windows in the Strand. For the same reason her own photograph – posed magisterial in her Sunday best and with her best bird-feathered hat tilted just so – was an imitation of one she had seen somewhere on display.

The photographs of Violet and Thomas showed they had become twins. The camera confirmed what Lucy had known from the beginning: they were matched physically and their union was arcanely inevitable. Both already looked a little older than in their wedding photographs; suffering had etched them, had given them a serious tone, had taken from them the light-heartedness of that day at Weller's house, blooming with expectation.

The failed photograph, and one that would distress everyone later on, was one that Jacob Webb had taken. Jacob insisted there should be a photograph which included Lucy, so he sensibly suggested a collective portrait. Lucy carefully set up the photographic apparatus, prepared the collodion, set the process in motion, and then took her place between Thomas and Mrs Minchin (holding Ellen), with Violet standing, to the left, at her husband's side. They were posed beneath a high arched canopy of leaves and the ambient light was diffuse and bright. However, Jacob at some point became anxious and confused; he was unsure of the principles of actual exposure. Lucy watched for a moment until, impatient and without thinking, she left the pose to help Jacob behind the lens. The result was that the others photographed clearly, but that Lucy, having moved during exposure from her initial position, appeared in print as blurred and residual. These pale diaphanous images photographers called "ghosts", and they were sometimes intentionally produced, Lucy had discovered, for the likes of Madame d'Esperance and Madame Noir. Jacob wished to try again, but Lucy refused.

Error and chance, she said. These are beautiful things. Clearly I am meant from now on to be a partickler ghost.

Thomas smiled sadly and kissed his sister: it was, Jacob thought, some kind of private joke. Something folded into families, something he had never experienced, knit them in special lexicons and private amusements.

In bed, later on, when they discussed the ghost, Jacob found Lucy stubborn. She would not pose again.

She was the instrument, she said, and not the subject. It was enough. It was her gift.

They made love in a luxurious and melancholy fashion. Jacob had learnt quickly the many ways to touch and enter Lucy, and she, in turn, knew many ways to receive him. They offered each other a correspondence of skin, widespread and generous. When they fell apart, each was varnished with sweat. Lovemaking had transfigured them.

"Marry me," said Jacob, still breathless and heaving.

But Lucy refused. She would never marry.

"You know I am ill."

"Then what", he persisted clumsily, "is to become of Ellen?"

"Mrs Minchin will be her mother," Lucy answered without pause. "Mrs Minchin will be a mother, after all."

"Do you not love me?"

"Love and marriage are not the same."

"I beg you," said Jacob.

But Lucy turned away. There was no way she could explain that she was entering her own eclipse, that it was hers alone, that she must prepare. Lucy felt Jacob's hand slide slowly along her hip and come to rest firmly on her shining thigh.

"I love you," he whispered.

"I know," she replied.

Lucy was more seriously ill than he guessed. She carried contagion deep within her. She had darkness in her chest, her own obscure chamber, and a presentiment not of dread, but of honourable mortality.

"When I was a child," Lucy said, changing the subject, "I owned a magnifying glass. It was a proud possession. I took it everywhere. But I didn't use it to see the magnification of things; I used it to burn. It astonishes me now."

"What?" asked Jacob.

"That I didn't know to see. Every blade of grass was a fuse. Every surface a temptation. I wanted ash, destruction."

She paused, remembering. Outside, an ash-coloured shine opened the morning.

Jacob lay silent.

"When I was a child," he said at last, "I believed the stories of the Bible. I believed in loaves and fishes, in walking on water. I believed in miracles."

Lucy waited.

"I even", he continued, "believed the story of Lazarus."

"And now?"

"Now nothing," said Jacob. "I believe in nothing but this." He touched Lucy's face gently, with his open hand.

58

JACOB AND LUCY WERE LOOKING AT PHOTOGRAPHS TOGETHER; SHE
was explaining what she called art-in-the-age-of-mechanical-
reproduction. They examined print after print, and Lucy spoke
of practised seeing, methodical execution, and all the positive
and negative relations that combine to conjure a beloved face.
Her images came in many colours – browns, purples, sepias,
olive – achieved by altering the developing silver with toning
solutions of other metals – gold, iron, copper, selenium. Lucy
was proud of her art: she saw before her an immanent
opulence, recorded as her own metaphysics. These images
would endure. These would gloriously outlive her.

"This one," said Lucy, pointing to a portrait of Violet
recovering, sitting by a window with a book in her lap, "this
one is special."

Jacob saw what he thought was a spoiled image. The right
side of the print was overtaken by a circle of white light, and
Violet was located to the left, as though cowering against glare.

"Halation, this is called. It is the halo of light that appears
around a bright object in a photograph – a window, a lamp, a
streetlight – which occurs in the printing process because of
excess light rays from the brilliant object reflecting back from
the emulsion support."

"A reflection."

"More than that, a flooding of light. A perceptible halo."

"A technical mistake."

"Yes, perhaps. The Royal College of Photographers would certainly deplore it. But it seems to me the loveliest accident. It shows us the force of radiance, its omnipresence."

"What you describe others would call the Holy Spirit."

"There are", she responded, wishing to teach him, "many kinds of spirit, many kinds of shrine."

"Halation." Jacob Webb repeated the word.

And for some reason he did not understand, he thought suddenly of his father. He had been a child of seven and looked truly for the very first time. He had seen his father immersed in a wave of clarity. He had looked death in the face and performed his own resurrection.

59

IN THE AUTUMN LUCY FELT HER BODY BEGIN TO FLINCH AGAINST THE chill air, which had an abrasive icy quality that seemed to cut away at her lungs. Enfolded in a crimson scarf, a matching woollen hat, gloves, and her old overcoat patchily lined with velvet, she was still assailed by the wind and defeated by the weather. Somehow she had already foreseen all this, that she would know surely when her last season had arrived, but that she would persist, as though ignorant, to place herself alive into the world. Lucy maintained her walks with Mrs Minchin and Ellen, striding against the pain and shortness of breath that gathered in her chest. She was weak and easily exhausted, and when she stopped for a rest her legs were wildly trembling and darkness swooped down upon her, in a momentary faint. Everywhere broad leaves were falling away, and Lucy had always enjoyed this process; the sky filling with blown colour and slow descending shadows. But now it seemed a disintegration. Mrs Minchin's concerned face bent above her, its purple somehow enhanced and flashing like a warning, and Ellen tugged at her hem to continue their excursion; but this time, this walk, Lucy could not go on. She felt herself fall sideways, blood leaking from her mouth.

When she woke Lucy found herself in bed, propped on huge pillows. Mrs Minchin sat beside her, darning a sock stretched taut over her competent fingers. Ellen, she explained, was with Thomas and Violet. Lucy knew herself to be in a state of high fever. She could feel her body burning intolerably so she flung off her bedclothes and tried to reach for the jug of water that stood close by on the side table. Mrs Minchin, who had never before seemed so purple or so very close, held her head and dabbed at her face with a damp cloth. She gave her sips of water and told her to sleep.

Time was elongated and then compressed in a concertina shape. Its pleats squeezed at Lucy's body, then stretched her into dreaming and delirium. Neither childhood nor future grew any less. She woke herself coughing. She felt a left-sided agony that seemed located at the heart. She reached instinctively to her throat and found there the cold Florentine beads that had belonged to her mother . . .

. . . Now it was Violet's turn to read.

"Let me see," she said, checking the spines of volumes before her.

Violet sat close by the bedside, a little alarmed that Lucy, who had only weeks ago been bossily instructing them to pose, was now chalk-coloured and supine, her face striated with blue veins. Lucy had requested Keats, but Violet thought that morbid. So she had chosen instead a Wilkie Collins, *The Woman in White*, a popular novel which promised to centre on romance and be sufficiently uplifting and diverting for one so ill. So she began the tale of Walter, the artist, and his love for the heroine, Laura, and soon fell entranced into the complex machinations of plot – the evil Sir Percival Glyde, the foreign villain, Fosco. Unaccustomed to fiction, Violet sank agreeably into the fakery and mischief of made-up people, the rigmarole of mean and devious motivation, the scheming against love. Lucy listened to her reading and heard Violet's voice quivering with excitement; she was charmed that her sister-in-law was so entranced by art.

Lucy had read the Collins novel before, and knew that Walter and Laura would end conveniently in each other's arms, that Fosco would be murdered and that Sir Percival would be burnt to death while tampering with a parish register to disguise his ignoble origins. But in her mind, now, the novel unplaited and reversed. The mysterious encounter with the woman in white, an enigma drifting out of the darkness with no identity and purpose, seemed to her especially poignant and compelling, and the end, not the beginning, of any story. Lucy closed her eyes against Violet's murmurous voice and saw herself, at midnight, meeting a woman in white, who might be her mother, or an Indian widow, or her own spooked self, a quivery pale presence, indistinct as water, something like the apparition screened on the ceiling, long ago, by Madame d'Esperance.

"Oh goodness me!" Mrs Minchin exclaimed, at some point in the narrative.

Lucy blinked open her eyes, and knew that the story had swollen into detail and kept moving on without her, and that she was transfixed, perhaps self-indulgently, by this single strange sign . . .

. . . She asked to be taken into the garden. Together Mrs Minchin and Violet lifted her onto a wheeled wicker chair and moved her, not outside – since it was raining – but to the back window. Lucy could see the rain-slicked path gleaming and orange leaves patterning the lawn. The trunks of the trees in the rain looked exceptionally dark, and were spotted with stains which resembled spilled silver nitrate.

Jacob was at her shoulder. He leaned across her for a kiss. Lucy could smell the tang of oil paint and see flecks and the open pores of his skin.

"Make love to me," Lucy whispered.

There was desperation in what she said, a plea, a complaint.

But Jacob halted, surprised, and replied that she must rest. He caressed her hot cheek with a single finger.

Perhaps I am repulsive, Lucy thought, my face a distortion, my body lean and contracted and vile with consumption. Perhaps I carry the sullen grimace of Her Majesty, Queen Victoria. She wanted nothing more than simply to encircle her lover, to call his name. She wanted him to lie with his head between her legs.

Jacob pulled up an armchair and sat beside her. Lucy could hear him speaking in kind and compassionate tones, dutifully chatting, but wanted touch, requited touch, not this extra disembodiment. She began to weep. Jacob was standing up, leaning over, concerned but unsure what he had said or done to upset her.

From somewhere Lucy remembered a word: ectoplasm. Perhaps it was the untouchable substance she was reverting to . . .

. . . She was waking from a dream, a dream about India. It was a heavy haul upwards, unswathing images. There were impossible entities, scraps of languages, distinct and mingled territories – all equally foreign – and the slow elucidation of an actual day. The dream exerted its pull even after the eyes were open. What gravity was it that weighed into this nether-world of broken images? In the future, Lucy decided, there will be a machine for recording dreams; sleepers would begin their day unburdened, knowing they could retrieve their dream-ings later on, awake, rational, open to every embedded message.

The sun had come out, undreamy, bright. There was a chorus of birdsong. In the garden the wet path was beginning to steam and patches of sunlight speckled the flowerbed like foxing on a print.

. . . She was now so hot that she must surely be incandescent. Her body glowed with its diseased and ghastly heat. Lucy was conscious that she was not dignified by her illness. She heard herself calling for Ellen — rudely and imperatively — and then could not bring herself to draw her near. This was no novelistic death-bed scene, with decorous wise words and shared understandings, swooning solemnity and whispered aphorisms, a hushed confession or two and a smiling final repose. She felt molten, inhuman. Lucy remembered the hectic blush that travelled her mother's body; she wondered what Ellen would remember, and asked that she be taken away.

But she had wanted, almost desperately, to speak to her daughter. She had wanted to draw her close. She had wanted to put her face at lover's distance, right to the child's ear, and say: "Your birth, my darling Ellen, your birth was remarkable, your birth was auspicious. There were forty, fifty, no, at least sixty lights . . ."

. . . Illness was a kind of flotation with no visible landfall, an unbecoming. People entered and left the room. Faces inclined towards her. She could feel a hand dampening her brow. She could hear quiet conversation. Oceans, dark oceans, stretched before her. There was a voice: "Drink this, drink just a little more . . ."

And there was another sound: swish-swish, swish-swish.

. . . After a short experience of exceptional pain, in which she imagined a spear of mirror penetrating her chest, Lucy became lucid. Her family was nearby. On the periphery of her vision she saw clearly Mrs Minchin, her expression beneficent. Ellen was curled on the bed, apparently asleep. Her face looked sealed off, lovely, safe. Just beyond stood Thomas and Violet, and Jacob Webb. There was no darkness she was heading to, no actual eclipse. There was just a slight tilt of vision, as when one tilts a daguerreotype in its box, and the image slides suddenly away, into shiny nothingness. Lucy closed her eyes, like the enlightened Buddha. Special things seen, and memories, and photographic prints, all converged to this quiet, private point. She tilted the glass. She was still anticipating images. She was still anticipating, more than anything, an abyss of light . . .

60

NOW, NOW. NOW, NOW.

Now that Ellen was a little older and much more settled, Thomas worried less. He still slept badly, from time to time, from an anguish he could neither decipher nor assimilate. Just one month after Lucy's death, Mrs Minchin had also died: a heart seizure, they said. It was so sudden, so final. The whole world changed shape. Ellen had come into their house, a confused and perplexed child, conscious of great unsayable loss, muted by all she could not understand. At first she was withdrawn and ill-behaved, and they found her hiding under beds, or crouching filthy in the coal cupboard. She spat food and tore at her clothes; she howled like an animal in the darkness. Jacob's regular visits had helped, and Violet's loving attention had finally won her over. They all adored her. She looked exactly, Thomas thought, as Lucy had as a small child and in his emotional extremity this added an extra confusion. Sometimes he caught himself calling the child by his sister's name.

Jacob had become prematurely grey, and appeared older than his thirty years and destroyed by grief. He was not coping well. If it had not been for Ellen, he confessed, he would have left this world with Lucy. It pained him that there existed only two photographs of his beloved. One was the ghost image, which the family could not quite bring themselves to dispose of, and the other was a studio photograph, taken in Bombay, in which Lucy stood posed beside Isaac Newton. She looked like a stranger, like a Mrs Newton, like someone unknown to them all. She was wearing unfamiliar clothes and had alien eyes. As her real face faded, slowly and imperceptibly, this false portrait would begin in sinister fashion to replace her. Jacob wished to paint an image from his sketches of Lucy, but was unmotivated, blank. He doubted his skill. He felt it an impossible task, to paint her luminosity.

Lucy had bequeathed to Jacob her Indian miniature – *The Lovers*, she called it. Jacob stared at the painting and found it childish, inept; it carried none of the nuance of oil paint and realistic portraiture. Yet something in the face of Radha subtly evoked Lucy's face. She had an intractable self-possession and a whispering gaze. On her chest were beetle wings, representing her flighty heart. Jacob rubbed his index finger on the wings and felt his own heart respond: some mystery of after-life momentarily possessed and moved him. In the absence of likeness there remained this trace of a touch, this memento of something actual but wholly unpictured. He woke from a dream in which his body was battered by hail.

At the Childish Establishment Thomas continued his projectionist work. Each night he watched as patrons surrendered to visions fantastical, and exclaimed, laughed, gasped and applauded. He worked the screening apparatus, the light effects and the sequencing of story. But his joy was gone. Thomas felt himself full of shabby, unresolved emotions; he felt suspended in a kind of absent-minded grief, which threatened to overtake and finally capsize him. Violet busied herself with the child, Ellen, but he hung back, inert, and somewhat unresponsive.

One day Thomas took to his bed – simply took to his bed

– to re-read *Great Expectations*. He read as carefully as possible, saturated by memories, and by the afternoon of the second day he was at the death-bed scene, in which the character Pip farewells his benefactor, the criminal, Magwitch. This is what Thomas read:

> He lay on his back, breathing with great difficulty. Do what he would, and love me though he did, the light left his face ever and again, and a film came over the placid look at the white ceiling.
>
> "Are you in much pain to-day?"
>
> "I don't complain of none, dear boy."
>
> "You never do complain."
>
> He had spoken his last words. He smiled, and I understood his touch to mean that he wished to lift my hand, and lay it on his breast. I laid it there, and he smiled again, and put both his hands upon it.

Thomas began to cry. He cried for his parents, for Neville and for Mrs Minchin. He cried for his cherished, irreplaceable sister, Lucy. He felt that the whole world was drenched in grief, and was unmanned, a boy again, a boy naked with a candle, fearing what might be screened unbidden on mirrors, or in dreams. Thomas was just moving beyond the vehemence of sobbing, just entering that state of calm and pause, when the bedroom door slowly opened before him. It was Ellen, seeking him out. She stood in a dusty diagonal beam of light, her small hand on the door, her attitude curious. Sensing, with an innate and precocious delicacy, that she had glimpsed something private, something she should not have seen, Ellen took a step backwards, very quietly, and pulled shut the door.

ACKNOWLEDGEMENTS

THIS BOOK WAS BEGUN DURING A WRITER'S RESIDENCY IN INDIA SPONSORED BY Asialink (Melbourne). I wish to express my heartfelt gratitude to my colleagues and friends at Asialink, an institution dedicated to cross-cultural understanding, tolerance, and the generation of artworks inspired by the honouring and celebration of cultural difference. My work with and for Asialink has been immensely enriching.

I was shown great kindness and hospitality in India and wish to thank, in particular, Ruchira, Ajit and Paroma Ghose, Anuradha Rao, and Maya and Mimansa Krishna Rao for their support. Esther Kinsky and Beth Yahp generously offered me writing spaces, as did Peter Bishop at the Varuna Writers' Centre. Special thanks to Susan Midalia for her perceptive comments on an early draft of the book, and to all my friends, particularly Victoria Burrows, who endured my endless disquisitions on anachronism and light. Zoë Waldie, of Rogers, Coleridge and White, has been enormously patient, helpful and diplomatic; without her assistance *Sixty Lights* would not have seen the light of day. Staff at Harvill have shown exemplary kindness, and Christopher MacLehose and Becky Toyne have offered unerringly clever and astute advice. My daughter Kyra, whose intelligence, sensitivity and fineness of spirit continue to inspire me, is at the very heart of this book.

The following texts have been especially useful in the composition of *Sixty Lights*. Lynda Nead's splendid *Victorian Babylon: People, Streets and Images in Nineteenth Century London* (Yale University Press, 2000), Eduardo Cadava's *Words of Light: Theses on the Philosophy of History* (Princeton University Press, 1997), Roland Barthes' *Camera Lucida: Reflections on Photography* (trans. Richard Howard, Flamingo, 1984) and Susan Sontag's *On Photography* (Penguin, 1979).